# The Secret Layer

## SIMMS THOMAS

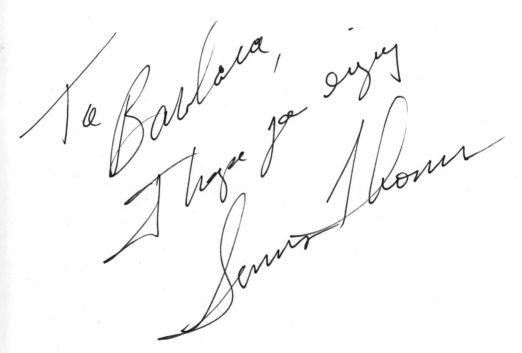

*To Barbara,
I hope you enjoy
Simms Thomas*

### SOUTHERN BOOK CLUB
Knoxville, TN

Published by the
Southern Book Club
Box 53112
Knoxville, Tennessee 37950

SouthernBookClub.com

For more information on Simms Thomas go to SimmsThomas.com

Comments and Letters:

Simms Thomas
C/O Southern Book Club
Box 53112
Knoxville, Tennessee 37950
Email: Simms@SimmsThomas.com

ISBN: 978-0-9801876-0-1

Set in Perpetua
Book Design by Daniel Middleton
www.scribefreelance.com

*Printed in the United States of America*

*To my closest women friends whom I know bury, hold on to, live and lie down each night with too many secrets. What an accomplishment to find the freedom in life when a secret means nothing and holds nothing on you.*

*Thanks to my husband who keeps my secrets, believes in me and was immensely helpful in making my first novel a reality.*

# Chapter One

EMILY WAS EXHAUSTED. Her fingers ached and her head hurt. But she was happy. She looked around her small bedroom littered with bits and pieces of every color of fabric in the rainbow. Yellow, black, and brown yarn lay in tiny balls at her feet. Small plastic eyes stared up blankly at the ceiling. Emily rubbed her own eyes and stretched.

Making her family and friends something for Christmas was giving her a great sense of achievement. Her grandmother had actually come up with the idea. She was the one person in the world Emily could always count on and she loved her more than anyone else in the world. Granny Millie was a tiny woman with tight white curls that lay flat against her head. She weighed all of one hundred pounds and stood just five feet tall. But she was a powerful woman, smart and bright. Emily would sit by her side for hours sharing all of her deep dark secrets. Not that she really had anything to tell. She would look into her beautiful sea blue eyes and pour out her confessions of love and hate. Her grandmother took her as serious as a heart attack, as she was fond of saying. She never laughed at Emily's confessions, only smiled and nodded before giving Emily deeply thought out advice.

Some thought her grandmother old and senile. But, Emily knew better. Emily closed her eyes and pretended her grandmother was sitting right there in her room. A smile crawled across her face. She knew her grandmother would stroke each doll and lovingly pat it on its yarn head and then tell her how proud she was of her.

Her grandmother heard everything and saw everything. Not much escaped her.

Her knowledge of current events had always impressed and fascinated Emily. She knew politics and had never missed the opportunity to step into a voting booth and pull that curtain as if it were the grandest thing on earth to do. She had voted through rain, shine, snow or sleet, threats of tornadoes and floods each and every election day since women had won the right back in 1920.

She was a staunch Democrat and really didn't care who the candidate was as long as he was a Democrat. She would support him fiercely and knew everything a candidate stood for along with his issues, his platform, his views, his wife's name and his children's names.

Granny Millie had lived with her family until late last summer and Emily missed her greatly. But, the "family" had decided it was best for the old woman to live with her mother's sister in South Carolina. Emily felt a tinge of sadness creep through her body. She wished she could hug her grandmother right now and smell the sweet lilac scent she wore. That smell always made Emily feel warm, wanted, and secure.

Emily shook her head. "Now, now, Em. Don't go tearin' up on me now." That's exactly what her grandmother would have told her. She thought of the upcoming summer visit with her grandmother in South Carolina. She was going to fly. Emily couldn't imagine what it was going to be like to soar through the air high above the world, flying with the birds. She knew she would love it because her grandmother had told her she would.

"Oh, 'tis a grand thing to fly my child. All of the houses look small as toys and cars are so tiny you'd think they were ants marching down the road. You never see people. Plain too small," her grandmother had said.

Emily picked up one of the rag dolls she had so meticulously crafted and sewn that day. She stroked its long strands of yellow hair with a certain pride and love, just as a mother would stroke her daughter's hair.

"I'll name you Lilly. And I'll make you a little necklace with your name stitched on it so you'll never forget."

Emily reached for her yarn, cloth, and sewing needle. With deftness and a skill beyond her twelve years, she sewed the name on the cloth. She brought the small square of fabric close to her eyes because the lettering had to be so small and exact. She could not chance missing a stitch. She smiled as she worked. She couldn't wait until her cousin, Mary Jo, opened her gift. She knew Mary Jo would love Lilly as much as she did.

Emily finished the doll's necklace and tied it around its neck. She gently placed the cherished piece in a box and wrapped the beautiful handmade gift of love with the paper from left over brown grocery bags. Emily used the remaining yarn to fashion a ribbon on the package. Carefully she wrote her cousin's name on the package.

Emily worked into the late hours finishing the dolls, placing each one lovingly in a box, covering it first with newspaper and then wrapping it with the brown paper from the store. Even with left over materials, Emily managed to make each package look festive. She glued stars and bells and angels on the boxes and carefully wrote her name to and from on each one. When the last one was finished, Emily tried to move her fingers.

"Ouch! This manual labor stuff is hard!"

Suddenly the quiet of the night made Emily feel very alone. Her mother had yelled good night to her hours ago after having a few cocktails. Emily knew she was snoring on the couch. She longed for her mother to just sit with her and talk. Just talk. "What did you do today in school, Emily?" "Who are your friends, Emily?" "What did you get on your math test, Emily?"

Was that too much to ask? She knew in her heart that would never happen. Emily's mother worked hard cleaning other people's houses in the little town of Sevierville, Tennessee. She took in laundry two days a week and was a seamstress in any spare time she happened to have. She was always working. Emily couldn't fault her mother for that.

Her thoughts drifted to her father. She wished she could be the little girl she saw in the magazines giving a welcome home hug and kiss to the tall man in the business suit after his long day at the office.

Emily's dad wasn't a large man, but he was built solid and could squeeze the life out of you with his tight muscles and hard callused hands. He had worked at Brogan's Chair Factory since he left school in the fifth grade. For some reason which Emily could not explain, she was proud of him. She really didn't care that he didn't wear a business suit.

He didn't even own a suit. She just really wanted more time with him. But he was like her mother. Always working and always tired.

Emily surveyed her day's work. She was satisfied and was more excited about giving her friends and cousins and grandmother the dolls than she was about getting anything for herself. She couldn't wait to hear their squeals of delight.

Emily truly couldn't remember when she had been happier. She crawled into bed with the doll she had made for herself.

"Oh Patsy, Santa will be here before we know it. Just seven more days then everyone can see your friends. And you will have someone to play with, too," Emily said sweetly to the doll she cradled in her arms.

Emily kissed her doll good night and like a beautiful young child on the verge of young womanhood, she sank into a deep peaceful sleep of dreams of her grandmother. They were laughing and cooking brownies, but something kept shaking her. Emily laughed at her grandmother, but the hand grabbed her again.

"EMILY, WAKE UP, EMILY," the voice said. "No, I don't want to," Emily begged. She didn't want to listen to the voice, but it persisted. The brownies and the dreams of a new Barbie doll slowly began to vanish.

EMILY'S TWO UNCLES, DELBERT and Roy, had spent the last four hours at the Elm Grove Tavern consuming a bottle of Jack Daniel's whiskey and chasing each shot with a bottle of beer. Nothing was unusual about this. This was routine for the pair and they were a familiar sight in the small town nestled in the foothills of the Great Smoky Mountains. They were the town's twin drunks who often ended their nights staggering down the street, holding onto each other, stumbling toward their rented trailer. But, this night, the wind whipped cold against their drunken breaths and they made it as far as their sister's house.

Delbert fumbled as he search for a key in his pocket while Roy looked under the torn straw mat on the front step and clumsily grabbed the spare key.

"This what ya lookin' fer?"

Delbert snatched it roughly away. "Don't be playin' games with me, you son of a bitch. I'm freezin' my ass off and here you are takin' the damn keys out of my pocket, you moron."

Roy started to respond but forgot he had just found the key. "Sorry, bro."

The pair tumbled into the small foyer. Marjorie's loud rhythmic snoring filled the air, causing the men to break into a rumble of snickering.

"Go Marjorie. Go Marjorie," Delbert chanted as he crawled up to his sleeping sister and threw the blanket over her.

"Check the fridge. Gotta be some brew in there," he ordered.

Roy managed a lopsided toothless smile, giggling, "Here drinky, drinky."

Delbert put his finger to lips, "Shhh. Don't be wakin' her up. Follow me."

Delbert tip-toed the best he could without falling down the hallway. Roy swayed, holding onto the walls for support as he followed Delbert and fell in step behind him. They opened Emily's door and slipped inside. Delbert pointed to her and a sickening grin spread across his face. Roy smiled and gave Delbert a thumb's up sign as he turned and locked the door behind him.

They staggered to Emily's bed. Delbert sat on the edge and took Patsy from Emily's slim arms. He tossed the newly made doll to Roy who immediately lifted its skirt, causing both of them to laugh. Delbert began shaking Emily, gently at first, then roughly.

Emily didn't know why the hand wanted to wake her from her wonderful dreams. She was tired and she and her grandmother were having fun. Emily could almost smell the brownies they were baking, but the hand continued to shake her. She laid there willing the voice to go away until she heard her uncle's voice telling her to awaken.

When she did, she didn't understand what was going on. Maybe they were there to tell her something had happened to her grandmother. But, she knew that wasn't true when she took a breath and smelled the pungent smell of liquor fill her room. She reached for her doll that Roy was playing with just as he began pulling Patsy's hair out. The two men giggled like school children.

"You don't need no dollies no more to play with. You a big girl now. Say bye-bye to dolls and hello to the real world. Why, we've come to change ya from a girlie to a woman, haven't we Roy?" Delbert cooed, keeping his hand firmly over Emily's mouth, using his other arm to bear down on her chest, pinning her to her bed.

Fear and bile rose in Emily all at once. She wanted to scream. She wanted to run. She needed to scream and run. She tried to free herself but it was useless.

"Oh come on Emmy. You gonna like it and you might as well get taught by family. 'Sides, we need ya to help us out tonight, don't we Roy?" growled Delbert, mean and low.

He glared into Emily's eyes and, seeing her fright, it excited him even more. Turning to Roy, he simply said, "This is gonna be fun."

Emily froze when the big dirty hand reached under her gown and pulled her panties down. She tried in vain to wiggle. She needed to free her arm. Just run and escape. Just move enough to scream, she thought. Surely her mother would hear her. Surely her father's shift at the factory would be over and he would come home and save her. Surely someone would help her. Time froze. No one came to her rescue.

BOTH MEN TOOK TURNS CRAWLING on top of her. Each would fumble at first then pump and grind and fondle her small breasts, bruising them. They squirmed and moved until Emily thought she would throw up and choke to death on her own vomit. The pain seared through to her very soul.

Then something in Emily died. She became very still and let them finish. They licked her and touched her and turned her over. Emily never knew a human being could be put through so much disgusting pain and yet still be alive. She was sure she was on the verge of death. She knew she was praying for death to come now and take her.

Her Uncle Roy watched his older brother grunting over the small clump of a child in her bed of pink and white flowers and lace trim. He spied the beautifully wrapped packages and began to unravel the yarn strings fashioned into bows. As Delbert groaned and moaned and slobbered all over Emily, Roy dismembered her dolls. When they were finished, both men gave each other a slap on the back.

Delbert leaned over close to Emily, almost touching her tear-stained face, whispering, "If you're a thinkin' you might want to share with someone 'bout tonight, I'd be thinkin' twice if I was you. If you so much as make a mention of this, I'll kill your precious grandma and your ma and then I'll bring my friends back 'round here to visit you a whole lot more. You understand girl?"

Emily didn't move. She just lay there. Roy and Delbert chuckled as Roy threw the destroyed rag dolls on top of the miserable child. Delbert burped loudly. Both walked out of her room with smirks on their faces, tiptoeing out the door as Marjorie continued to snore loudly, never knowing anyone had ever entered her house.


EMILY WAITED FOR DEATH to come. She thought she might have lain there, uncovered and bleeding for hours. She didn't know if she could move. She was cold. Her body had become a stone. It ached as the blood dried on her. Trying to move, the pain gripped her with a force that sucked her breath away and she clutched her small body. Slowly, she swung her feet over her bed. With a will and determination and a show of strength worthy of great souls, Emily made her way to the small bathroom.

As she weakly edged her way in the darkness, Emily reached out in search of the shower. She climbed inside and shut the door, turning the water on as hot as she could stand it on her bruised and ravaged skin. She stood under the steaming water as it burned her flesh.

Finally, tears fell and sobs escaped her mouth. She was an animal in a cage. Never had anything hurt so much. Emily crumpled to the shower stall floor and wailed. With clinched fists, she vowed she would not tell anyone what had happened to her. This would be her secret and hers alone. She shivered as she held her knees close to her chest and wondered how she was going to handle the enormity of this secret. The only certainty in her mind at that agonizing moment was that this was never going to happen to her again.

# Chapter Two

EMILY OPENED HER EYES and let them adjust to the light around her. The sun filtered through the heavy navy blue damask curtains, casting long shadows across the room. For a brief moment she only stared at the unfamiliar ceiling above her. She noticed how glitter danced across the ceiling. The white and silver sparkles reminded her of fairy dust.

Emily drew the stiff white sheets closer to her chest as she studied the room around her. The avocado colored shag carpet and dark grain wood of the dresser and end tables soaked up most of the strands of sunlight entering through the curtains. The room was clean but sparsely furnished. The queen bed took up most of the space. She scrutinized the wide yellow and green stripes of the bedspread, thinking she would never have chosen such a pattern. Tacky came to mind. The flowered wallpaper featured the same bright green and yellow colors. Each flower was the size of a large dinner plate and made the room appear smaller than it actually was. The nicest feature of the room was a small sitting table with a large beveled mirror that sat in the corner.

When she had entered the room the night before, Emily had thought the table oddly out of place. It was almost elegant, with its pale yellow lace skirt hiding its legs. Emily had carefully laid all of her toiletries on the table's glass top before preparing for bed. A sly and beautiful smile slid across her lovely face. She swung her long limbs from the hotel bed, arching her back, stretching. She raked her perfectly manicured fingernails through her golden mane of hair. This was the day she had been plotting, planning, and dreaming of since she was twelve years old and had taken that fateful plane trip to South Carolina.

Emily closed her eyes again as the sweet memories returned for the millionth time. She smiled as thoughts of her summer of freedom and discovery sailed through her mind. She remembered how frightened she had been when the plane's door had shut. Her body trembled ever so lightly. She had taken a deep breath and then the plane had lifted off the ground. She was flying. Fear evaporated from her body and a feeling of freedom had been so strong that Emily had been giddy with excitement.

Seven years ago. It seemed like yesterday, Emily mused. Her grandmother had been right. Flying was a beautiful awakening of the soul, and it was made for beautiful people.

Emily had met her destiny on that short plane ride the moment the raven haired exotic airline stewardess asked the then coltish beauty if she would like a soda. Emily had stared back, mouth agape. The woman's perfectly coifed hair. The crisp starched red and yellow uniform hugging her shapely body.

Emily noticed the respect the woman demanded and got from everyone on the plane, and all she had asked was what those people had wanted to drink! Emily breathed the air around her, remembering the fragrance that had stirred through the air. It reminded her of the sweet scent of roses from a beautiful garden at dusk when the smell is full and bold.

Yes, Emily had known at that moment she wanted to be assured, confident, beautiful—the queen of the sky. Today, nearly seven years to the day, Emily Anderson's dream was coming true. Today was her first day at Pacific Airlines.

She hastened her step, opening her suitcase once more to check the items neatly folded inside. Each suit was wrapped in pale blue tissue paper. There were only a few items, but Emily didn't care. She knew only good things were in store for her. She let her fingers glide over the delicate fabric of the crisply starched uniform she would wear everyday, and she smiled. She didn't need a lot of other clothes. She had invested her money wisely and had all that she needed. Anyone who ever saw her clothes would know they were expensive.

Emily had put not only time and effort but a lot of thought into the selection of her wardrobe. She had purchased three suits, all in rich dark colors of burgundy, navy, and black; one pair of wool gabardine fully lined charcoal slacks, and a lighter silk blend cream pair; one fine cotton white shirt; one sky blue silk blouse with hidden buttons; and a cashmere sweater set that was the most exquisite mint green color she had ever seen.

Her one dress would be noticed by anyone who ever came within fifty feet of her when she had it on. It was made of pure silk and draped her slender shoulders before layering into a V at the small of her back, thus showing-off her taut muscles. It fell seductively over her hips and hung just below her knees. The floral pattern of spring bouquets in colors of mints, lilacs, pinks, and creams barely showed because they were so pale.

Everything coordinated perfectly. Her new blouse and shirt could be worn with any of her suits. Her cashmere sweater could be worn around her shoulders with her dress. The white crisp shirt could go with any of the slacks.

Of course, Emily had an unmistakable flair for fashion unequal to anyone she knew. She didn't know where the talent came from, but it had always been natural and easy for her to mix and match, sew and put together things. And it always appeared to have been completed by a professional.

So what if she had to take all of her graduation money, sell all of her old clothes, use her grandmother's small "inheritance money," as Emily called it, to buy the new clothes. They were worth it. And so was she, she thought.

Emily began her mantra to herself, "I'm fulfilling a dream and dreams don't come cheap." She smiled at her own wisdom and sat down before the mirror to start her strict ritual of applying her makeup.

Emily again arranged her makeup in front of her on the small dressing table and stared at her reflection. She was beautiful, she guessed. Everyone said so.

Shrugging her shoulders she thought about other girls her age back in Sevierville, Tennessee. Most would get married, have dozens of children and get fat with a homegrown boy. But Emily Anderson had never wanted that kind of life. She had plans, and they were very specific plans.

The first step had already been taken. She was going to be an airline stewardess. The reflection staring back at her was radiant. The smile broadened as she thought how easy it had been. Emily had never been like the girls back home.

It seemed ages ago now, but it actually had only been a few short months before when her friends had laughed at her when she had taken the bus into Knoxville for a day of beauty.

She had watched the woman at the makeup counter applying makeup all day before her own appointment time. Usually they spent forty-five minutes with each client. But with Emily it was different.

She may have been just shy of twenty, but no one said no to Emily. It was her turn. She was the client. And she was very precise in her needs and wants. She had not liked the first colors the young artist had put on her face. And to the woman's surprise, Emily had been right. They worked together using different colors, hues, and combinations until the makeup was perfect. Two hours had passed and the makeup artists had to admit that not only had Emily been correct in her vision of makeup for herself, she had transformed into a beautiful creature.

Emily had purchased everything she needed for her own makeup kit that day, not once paying attention to the costs. Money would not stand in her way of achieving her goals. You had to spend money to make money. You had to spend money to make a life, too.

EMILY TILTED HER HEAD AND PUCKERED her lips, making herself laugh out loud. She had followed the plan for her life as one might follow a map. Never once had she wavered from her goal. Her thoughts drifted as she remembered her journey to this day.

IT WAS LAST SPRING WHEN SHE had taken the trip to Nashville. Stopping at every little dusty town from East Tennessee to Middle Tennessee had taken eight hours on the bus. But, Emily had been wise to give herself a full four days for the trip.

That too had been easy. Her mother thought she was going on a camping trip with friends. Her friends thought she was visiting relatives and would be out of town for a few days. No one was the wiser. No one was dumber, Emily thought. She had never before expressed an interest in camping and she never spoke of any relatives since her grandmother's death.

It had taken Emily less than an hour to find the most expensive dress shop in Nashville. Just reliving how she had twirled in front of the big three-paneled mirror trying on dress after dress made Emily's heart swell with pleasure. Her five foot eight inch slim frame made each dress come alive. On anyone else the dresses would have looked simple. Not on Emily. Most took on an elegance of their own, not seen before.

With Emily's keen eye for fashion and detail she selected her one dress. Many would have guessed that the dress was from a private salon in New York, or even Paris. Most of it had to do not with the dress itself but with how Emily wore it, with a style and grace befitting a princess. She had then selected her suits and other items. Even the suits created a regal presence when she put them on.  On anyone else, the suits most likely would have looked ordinary. She could never wear anything so stylish or beautiful in the tiny Tennessee town she so desperately wanted to leave so very far behind.

After catching the bus, Emily had made the trip back across the state and, passing right through Sevierville, she headed to Charlotte, North Carolina to the Pacific Airlines East Coast office. From the moment she entered the small, cluttered office, she knew she was in control of the situation. She wasn't nervous. She wasn't afraid. She was only going through the motions to fulfill the dream.

The office furniture was battered, old, and had seen many other offices before it had landed there. Most of the desks were scratched and dented. The chairs squeaked and the chocolate brown shag carpet needed cleaning. The paisley print wallpaper was fraying and peeling and smoke filled the air. But, to Emily it was a palace and smelled of sweet perfume.

The General Manager never knew what hit him when Emily breezed into his office and flashed her perfect white teeth and had truthfully cooed, "All I've ever really wanted in life is to work for Pacific Air."

Paul Brady was overweight, balding, squat and in need of a breath mint.  His shirt was wrinkled and a size too small, his tie was askew. He quickly found himself sucking in his gut and straightening his tie. He swallowed hard, trying not to look at the long legs crossed in front of him.

He almost thought he had licked his lips when he looked at Emily. Emily just stared at him, never letting her azure eyes leave his gaze.

"Do I qualify, Mr. Brady? I just graduated from high school and I've taken some correspondent courses from The University of Tennessee. But, all I really and honestly want to do is be a part of your team."

Clearing his throat and trying his best to gain some composure, Paul Brady tried to speak in a steady tone.

"We do have an opening. You would fly the northwest cities for six months, be on six days, off three days. Of course, you'd have to be on reserve, as we call it, for twelve months. That pretty much means you stay by the telephone. Not much of a social life because you have to be ready to fly when you get the call. But, I'm getting ahead of myself."

Paul Brady had been ahead of himself the second Emily had walked through his door. He droned on, "First, you stay here in Charlotte and complete the course work, and of course, pass the test." He hoped he didn't sound like a dirty old man, not that lewd thoughts weren't racing through his brain. How he would love to run his hand over her smooth young skin, reach under that elegant suit and see what true beauty was all about. It was then that he realized Emily had spoken to him and he shook his head to clear his thoughts, "I'm sorry dear, you were saying?" Emily clearly read his mind and she didn't care.

"All I was saying is that I would be thrilled to stay in Charlotte. It's a fascinating city. I was just wondering if you would be able to help me find a place to stay and maybe show me around?"

Paul had to catch his breath. Was this glorious creature coming on to him, or was she truly an innocent naive young woman in a jungle of men and evil thoughts? Paul remained steady.

"The company provides lodging. All of the girls stay together. The three-week course starts two weeks from Monday. I can show you around this afternoon if you like, unless, that is, you need to return home and discuss this with your parents and get back with us."

Emily held back a laugh and almost choked. Discuss it with her parents? He must think of her as a child. Well, she could change that soon enough if she needed to.

"My parents have already given their consent, thank you. But, yes, I do need to return home and take care of a few financial matters."

Paul Brady tried to size up this beautiful headstrong young woman sitting before him. Financial matters? What financial matters could such a young person have to clear up? It was of no concern to him. He just knew he wanted her around, even if it would be for just a few short weeks.

"Yes, that would be just fine. Welcome aboard. I have the feeling you're really going to love your job," Paul stated.

"You have no idea, just no idea," enthused Emily.

That's all it had taken. The bus trip home seemed to take days, but Emily had a new glow about her.  Her spirit was alive and her outlook on life was good. She felt pure joy.


SHE RELISHED THE CHORE ahead. Emily bounded into her room and began taking every single item out of her closet and drawers. Carefully she folded them after pricing each item.  She wanted no reminder of this life she had lived. Nothing was spared, for nothing truly held a fond memory. Not any more. Not for a long time.

Emily boxed up her stereo, radio, and the ice blue taffeta prom-dress. She stopped briefly and thought about her prom.  Jerry Scott, a nice sweet boy with startling jade green eyes and curly jet black hair, had been her date. He had been so nervous pinning on her corsage that he had brushed her breast. His face had turned a deep crimson and he had been rendered speechless.  Emily had not been angry. She hadn't been embarrassed. She had felt pity for the boy who would live his life out in that small town, following in his father's footsteps by selling shoes at his family's store. The dress would be one of the first items to sell.

Emily worked well into the night preparing for the garage sale.  She wanted no reminders of this life. She was ready to move forward.

Since the first month that her grandmother had moved away, until six months ago when she died, Granny Millie had sent her a little card with the same note: "My dear Em. Here's a little bit of spending money. Buy yourself something extra pretty." But Emily had never spent one penny. She had saved every dollar bill that came to her. She knew the sale of her possessions wouldn't bring in a lot more, but it would be a decent nest egg to start with, coupled with the balance of her grandmother's money.

The day of the sale was a typical crisp East Tennessee fall morning. The mist hung heavy over the Smoky Mountains as they took on shades of purple and blue. A light frost danced across the yellow and orange leaves that still clung to life and trimmed the Oak and Maple trees as winter called to them to change. Yes, it was a season for change and Emily was ready for the change.

The sale went well, and what didn't sell, Emily hauled to the Goodwill bin in the town's center. She marched over to the bank and closed her savings account. It was a bittersweet ending.

Emily had always had her own private dream. She would save her money until she could find the perfect little house to buy for her and her grandmother. The two of them would cook, sew, laugh, and dream together

Then, her life would be redeemed in some way, she felt. The terrible abuse she had suffered would be easier to live with each day, because it had given her the strength to nurture a goal and dream. But, that dream had died with her grandmother. She knew in her heart that her grandmother was watching over her. She would make her proud. She would not keep looking back and remembering. "Move forward," she whispered.

Now she looked at her new wardrobe that the money had helped buy. With tender loving care she wrapped each piece of clothing and placed the articles in her new red vinyl American Tourister luggage set. She shut the suitcases and had but one thing left to do. She had to tell her parents she was leaving on the six o'clock bus to Charlotte to start a new job. Goodbye. So long. See you in another life.

It had not been difficult. Neither parent had tried to stop her because they had known she was lost to them. They just didn't know why.

PACIFIC COAST AIRLINES EAST COAST Division held its training in a modern five story office complex in the heart of Charlotte. Emily found herself facing Paul Brady for the first four days for lunch. She heard the whispers and felt what she thought were undercurrents of jealousy being directed her way. But, by the end of the first week, most of the girls realized it wasn't Emily that deserved to be ridiculed. It was plain to see that it was Paul Brady who was making a fat fool out of himself.

Emily politely excused herself a few minutes before the lunch break on the fifth day. Instead of going into the ladies' room, she quietly slipped through the exit door, entered the stairwell, and walked out of a side door into the bright sunshine of the city. The other girls had laughed conspiratorially as they retold the story of Paul Brady waiting impatiently for Emily outside of the ladies' restroom, pacing, for 45 minutes.

For the next two weeks, Emily left the classroom with large groups and would wave to Paul.

"I'm loving the classes and learning so much," she would say in passing, pretending to be so engrossed in conversation with her fellow students that he didn't dare to single her out. Sometimes she simply said she had a headache and felt like being alone. On two occasions, Emily brought her own lunch and stated that she had to study.

But, Emily wasn't stupid either. She knew better than to completely alienate the man. After all, he could help her. So, she was coy and slightly flirtatious. She kept Paul at a close yet safe distance for the remainder of her stay.

The night of graduation finally dawned and Emily was surprisingly giddy. All of her hard work was paying off. She once again thought of her mantra. "I'm fulfilling my dreams. Dreams do not come cheap," she repeated. Sighing deeply, she left her hotel room to attend the ceremonies and to face Paul Brady once again.

Paul stood outside the auditorium door with a small bouquet of roses. He was a puppy dog in love and he didn't even care who saw him. Emily cared and she cringed as she accepted the flowers and thanked him.

"Paul, you really shouldn't have. All of the other girls will be jealous. Please don't."

"Oh, just let old Paul worry about all that."

"Well, thank you for all of your help, and your kindness. You've been like a brother to me. Here. I have something for you." Emily handed Paul a slender box wrapped in beautiful silver blue foil.

"Paul, I don't know what I would have done without you. You have become my friend and mentor and I truly thank you."

Opening it, he found a Cross pen set with the words, "Thanks to my friend" engraved on the side. Paul looked up at Emily as he put the gift in his pocket.

"Friend. Brother. Mentor. You're really throwing them out there tonight aren't you, Em."

Emily replied by staring straight into his eyes. "I have no idea what you're talking about."

Paul only waved his hand over his head as he started toward his seat. "I'll see you later, Em. See you later."

Emily sat ramrod straight during the exhausting ceremony. The auditorium was hot and overcrowded. Emily was looking forward to the cold glass of champagne during the reception.

"Emily, I hope we get on some flights together," one of the girls enthused.

"Yes, that would be nice, but who knows where our routes will be? Have you heard anything?"

"No. From what I hear, we start at the bottom of the food chain and work our way up. Who cares? We are certified," the young woman said, as she waved her certificate in the air.

"Oh, I wouldn't worry too much about your schedule," Paul Brady hissed into Emily's ear. She jumped as he slipped up behind her and gently grabbed her elbow, directing her toward the door.

"Wouldn't you like a glass of champagne to toast me, Paul?" Emily glanced over her shoulder to see if anyone was watching.

"It can wait. I want to celebrate with you privately," he said, as he guided her through the door and to his waiting car. Emily slid into the front seat. Paul rounded the corner of the car quickly and leaned in close to her.

"Em, don't play games with me. I know you may not know it, but you want me." His fat fingers strummed her leg then slowly started crawling up her thigh. Emily felt lightheaded. She took a deep breath to steady her thoughts, which Paul mistook for pleasure. "See? I knew you'd want it."

His hand reached her panties and he tried to slip his fingers underneath the sheer silk garment.

"Paradise awaits me," he groaned. Emily froze. Her mind raced. She reached down and put her hand firmly on top of Paul's, denying him access to her.

"Not here, Paul. Not tonight. I don't want to remember you, or us, like this."

Emily fought to hold back tears noticing the bulge in Paul's pants.

She didn't know if he heard her. His hand remained under her dress and right at her panty line. He gently stroked the outside of her panties. His finger lifted the elastic strap of the undergarment.

"Paul. Someday it will happen. It will be right at that time. Not in some car. Not like this." His finger slipped under the garment and Emily bolted violently erect. Paul stroked her once, and then slowly removed his hand.

"Okay, Em. Someday it will happen. You just remember that ol' promise when I call to collect." He brought his fingers to his nose and inhaled her scent deeply. "Lucky fingers. Next time it will be my tongue."

Emily swallowed hard. She smoothed her dress down and looked around to see if anyone had been watching. She wanted to kill Paul Brady. She truly wanted to take her bare hands and strangle him. But she knew she still needed him. He could make or break her schedule right now. Emily had to continue the game and play her cards right.

"Who knows where I'll be sent. I may never see you. I do know that I'm the low man on the totem pole. I'm so nervous about my assignment. Not knowing where I'm going to be sent or who I'm going to be around." She was rambling, but she didn't care. She wanted out of the car.

Paul sat up and straightened his crotch. "Don't worry your pretty little head over that. Old Paul will always take care of you. Why, I feel like I discovered you, and I can't wait to really discover you, if you know what I mean."

Emily could only manage a weary smile. She wanted a good schedule. She wanted to advance quickly.

She gently squeezed his arm, thanking him, as a sickening feeling grew in the pit of her stomach. She knew that one day she would have to cross the bridge of Paul Brady and burn it to the ground. Torch it. But not just yet.

The walk down memory lane brought Emily quickly back to reality, as she finished the last expert strokes of her makeup brush and critically surveyed the work. She liked what she saw.

She swept her golden hair into a tight bun, leaving a few tendrils to frame her lovely face. She had beautiful features. Her eyes were large and her lashes long, silky, and full. Her lips were swollen with their fullness.

She thought about the last four weeks of her life. It seemed to her that men had only wanted her body and her face all of her life.

For a brief moment she let her mind drift back to her bedroom when she was twelve years old and her two uncles had entered her room. After that night, she knew she would hold her head high, do what she had to do and never let a man take control of her again. And she hadn't.


EMILY'S THREE YEARS AT SEVIERVILLE High School had been good. She had been popular in school and well liked, although she never formed any close relationships with girls or boys. She was head cheerleader and class president and dated the captain of the football team. Her beauty had won her the titles of Miss Sevierville and Miss Sevierville High Queen. But, not one boy ever touched her. She knew they all secretly called her the Ice Maiden. But, she also knew they respected her. If only they knew the memories of what she went home to. But no one would ever know about that. Not yet, at least. One day, Emily dreamed, they would pay for the childhood they had taken away from her. But it had been her and her alone that had instilled some sort of normalcy in her life. Again, once she took control, her life was better.

Emily knew she always had to be in control. If she ever gave that control up, trouble would follow. So, on that humid but beautiful summer day years ago—when Emily boarded the plane to South

Carolina to see her precious grandmother—she had all of her questions answered. All it took was that one trip to know what she wanted in life. Her dream had been born and she had raised it ever since. Now that dream was almost grown. She was tired of hiding behind it. She was tired of always having to escape to the dream. Now she didn't have to escape. She was here. Within an hour, she would be on a plane to take her to a new city to live with three other girls from other cities across the country. They didn't know her and she didn't know them. She was ready to live her dream. Emily gently pinched herself to make sure she wasn't asleep.

PAUL BRADY HAD BEEN smart enough to assign Emily far away from him for the time being. He thought it made perfect sense for her to have a fantastic route for maybe six months, tops, and then get her back close to him. That way, no one could ever figure out his ultimate goal of having Emily at his beck and call.

Emily's home base city was Seattle, Washington. Most people think of Seattle as just a rainy city, miserable. But, actually, that isn't true. The city's annual precipitation is less than all of the major eastern seaboard cities. The difference is Seattle gets most of its precipitation in the form of rain, while other cities across the country get rain and snow. But precipitation is precipitation. Seattle is gloomy, though. From May through October the skies are usually more clouds than sun and in the spring, the marine layer hovers over the land for a good part of the morning to midday.

But, on the clear sunny days, even if they may be few and far between, it is a spectacular city. Since Seattle is bordered by and dotted with bodies of water, and because it is a city of hills, the views from many areas are in plain site. To the west is Puget Sound, an inland salt water sea that flows out through the Strait of Juan de Fuca into the Pacific Ocean. To the east is twenty two miles of Lake Washington, a clean mountain-fed lake close to sea level. And in between The Sound and Lake Washington is Lake Union.

Downtown Seattle is on a steep hillside rising away from a cliff just above Puget Sound. Emily hoped the apartment she would share would be somewhere close to that area. She wanted to see the water on each day that was possible. Of course, she also knew it would be just as nice on First Hill, Capital Hill, Queene Anne, or Beacon Hill. She also knew she wouldn't be there much anyway.

Emily was told her three roommates wouldn't see one another very often, as their schedules would be different. Emily put the perfectly starched, tight fitting skirt, blouse, and jacket on. She attached the airline wings to her suit coat and a wave of excitement coursed through her body. Almost reverently she placed the navy blue hat on her head, tilting it ever so slightly. She gathered her makeup and gently placed the bag next to her wrapped suits and clothing. Emily rubbed her hand over the fine tissue paper and smiled, "You are well worth the investment. To look expensive is half the battle. To carry it off is another. I plan to do both!" Emily was ready to face, and conquer the world. She snapped the suitcase shut and headed out the door, leaving the old Emily behind.

# Chapter Three

EMILY NODDED PLEASANTLY TO several passengers as she made her way toward the rear cabin of the plane. "I've got two rum and cokes, one vodka straight up, and one beer, Patty. Can you handle those for me? I've got to go work first class."

Patty looked at Emily and rolled her eyes. "Sure. You go work first class Emily. Leave me back here collecting money and passing the peanuts to the apes."

Emily laughed, waving as she walked with grace down the plane's narrow aisle. "Always the comic. Always the comic."

Emily eased the heavy red velvet curtain panel back and slipped into the first class section. Ten men lined the aisles in dark business suits. Emily loved working the first class section. Not only did she meet interesting men and have wonderful intellectual conversations, but she even got good business tips at times.

Daniel Orasy, a forty-five year old stock broker, who was obviously quite successful in his Savile Row tailored suits, had suggested she invest in a computer company. It had been refreshing to him when Emily confided that she didn't know how to go about it. Most people wanted others to think they knew everything. Not Emily. She was honest and forthright and Daniel liked that quality in her. He was more than willing to help.

Emily had met him three days later at his office, where he set up an account for her. He painstakingly took her through the steps and suggested several stocks. Emily studied the information he had gathered for her and then wrote a check for every penny she could afford. Daniel had first been taken aback by her sheer beauty, but now it was her intellect that he so admired. Within six months, her investments had increased by threefold. She and Daniel spoke often and had become good friends, but she kept a business edge to their friendship. Emily had decided early on that pleasure and business and her job needed to remain separate. Each investment was pure gold to Emily. Daniel was happy for her and pleased with himself. In the back of his mind he thought that maybe one day Emily would want to show her gratitude toward him in a different way. But even as the thought had formed, he knew, deep down, that he was sadly mistaken.

EMILY PASSED THROUGH THE aisle distributing drinks when a husky voice sliced though the cabin.

"Excuse me sweetheart. When you get a moment, I would truly like a gin and tonic. Very little ice and a lime twist." Emily slowly turned, wanting to find the face that belonged to the voice that commanded attention yet was gentle and soft and smooth like velvet. It had a husky tone, but also a coolness that took Emily's concentration away, let alone her breath.

Emily felt like she was moving in slow motion as she turned and faced the most handsome man she had ever laid her eyes on. He was an Italian Stallion, a Greek God, and a well sculpted Roman statue all in one. He was every woman's dream of a man. His thick black hair waved ever so slightly. His cobalt blue eyes danced with laughter. His well toned muscular body filled his expensive handmade suit to perfection. His teeth were white and bright and perfect. And he was staring at her with a bemused look on his face.

"Did I say something wrong, Miss?"

Emily continued to be mesmerized by this creature.

"Can I get that drink before we land?"

Emily suddenly realized her face was turning a crimson color, and then she felt the color drain from her face completely. He was talking to her, and she was standing in the aisle holding a drink tray and not moving.

"I'm sorry, Sir. Of course you can get that drink. What would you like? No. You told me. You want a...a...a..."

Coming to her rescue, the man just smiled and quietly restated his request. "A gin and tonic with very little ice and a lime twist."

Emily felt some of the color returning to her cheeks. "Of course. I'll get that right out for you."

Emily would have jumped hurdles to escape the man's stare. She hastened her step and almost threw herself behind the curtain. The other stewardesses stopped preparing drinks and looked at Emily.

"My God, you look like you've seen a ghost," Susan said.

Emily took a deep breath. "Sitting in row four, seat A, is the best looking man I have ever laid my eyes on in my entire life. His voice is a warm river flowing slowly down a mountain. His eyes are pools of jewels. His looks are movie star quality. His clothes are from Milan, or somewhere, and I couldn't do anything but stare with an open mouth. I am so embarrassed."

Susan peeked through the curtain. "Well, if it's a problem, I'll take him the drink."

Emily reached for a fresh glass. "Not on your life."

Eve had to see him too. As she pulled the curtain back, Emily smacked her hand, and said, "No! He might see us. If we hit turbulence and I spill this all over him, I am positively jumping out of this plane." Then Emily slid through the curtain to deliver the man his drink.

Eric Blake kept his eyes trained on Emily. He knew a beauty when he saw one. He also knew class when he saw it. And Emily oozed class and beauty. Yes, this was one woman he wanted to get to know. God only knew how many eager beavers he had run into lately, only to find they couldn't hold a conversation and had absolutely nothing to offer him. Eric Blake needed a lot from a woman. This one may be an airline stewardess, but he could smell success and upbringing. By the time Emily finally reached him with his drink, Eric had every intention of getting to know her very well, very well indeed.

Emily tried her best to remain calm, cool, and collected. She was one with the plane, gliding through the air. "Here you go. One gin and tonic. Very little ice and a twist of lime. Can I get you anything else?"

Eric flashed her a million dollar smile that immediately began to melt her heart.

"As a matter of fact, you can. You see, I have never been to Seattle. Is this your base city?"

Emily couldn't believe her ears. "Yes. I've lived here for about seven months. It's a great city, you'll love it."

Eric was smooth. He knew not to rush anything. Timing was everything. "Well, I'm sure I would love it more if I had a tour guide for the day. Would you be available to show me some of the sights?" Emily swallowed hard and nodded her head, afraid of her own voice.

She had never been in love. She had never let herself feel anything for a man. She had always been cool and in control. Yet, here was a man who, within five minutes, had literally taken her breath away. She wondered if this was what love was like. Love at first sight.

Never missing a beat, and never revealing her inward delight, Emily smiled and calmly replied. "I would love to show you around the city. Just let me know where you're staying and I can meet you there."

Eric shook his head. "No, I will send a car for you and we will go have breakfast. Perhaps plan our whole day. Does that sound agreeable to you?"

Emily thought if she died right now, she would die happy.

"Most agreeable. By the way, my name is Emily Anderson."

Eric extended his hand in an almost formal way, taking her hand in his, and locking eyes with hers.

"And my name, Mademoiselle, is Eric Blake. And you are quite lovely, Miss Anderson. I look forward to tomorrow's outing."

Emily gently eased her hand from his. "I'll write my address down for your driver. Is nine o'clock okay for you?"

Teasingly, in his best genie voice, Eric replied, "Your wish is my command."

Emily's eyes danced as she turned to walk toward the stewardess' station. Susan grabbed her, almost causing her to fall. "Tell me everything. Is he ga ga over you? Are you going out? Please say you're going. What am I saying? Say you're not going out and he is really crazy about me!"

Emily laughed. "Yes. We're going out. His 'driver' is picking me up at nine in the morning."

Susan put her hand to her mouth.

"Oh my God. He must be loaded. You lucky little girl."

The words caught Emily by surprise. "It's about time," she whispered.


EMILY'S APARTMENT WAS SURPRISINGLY spacious and, with a side view of the sound on one side (on a day that wasn't overcast), one could see the top of the Space Needle, which, at this particular moment, was shrouded by dense gray clouds. The one thing she could always count on in Seattle was overcast skies, or rain. Fortunately, today was nice by Seattle standards.

The room was sparsely furnished, but large. There were three bedrooms, a living room-dining room combination, and two bathrooms. Emily had been lucky enough to get the bedroom with the bathroom. The previous girl had suddenly been transferred to the East Coast Route. She knew that Paul Brady had most likely played a hand in that decision.

The other two girls, Nancy and Joy, had been living there for eight months before Emily arrived. Both had stated that they were too settled into their own rooms to vacate them, but Emily had often wondered if they had ever been given a choice. She liked her roommates, but she didn't have anything in common with them, except for work. On the rare occasions when they ended up at the apartment together they would cook, watch TV, and talk shop. She, of course, liked it best when she had the place to herself. Generally, her home was a hotel room up and down the northwest coast. Sometimes she got lucky and flew to Chicago. Whenever that happened, she went shopping.

Emily was very careful with her money and what she bought. If it wasn't the absolute best, then she didn't buy it. She would rather have one good pair of slacks than five cheap pairs. She made sure every article of clothing was first quality, top of the line, and usually designer best. Her shoes were few, but they would last forever. When she had spent one hundred dollars on a small purse she didn't even blink an eye.

Her roommates envied her beautiful clothes. And only once did one of them ask to borrow something to wear. Emily had nicely but firmly told her that she never lent her clothes out, as part of a rule she had established since she was a child. Whatever the reaction from the roommates, the answer had been understood.

Emily looked around her bedroom, which was devoid of any real personality. It consisted of a bed, a small dresser, and dressing table. She knew that when the time came for her to buy the things she truly needed and wanted, she would be ready-- unlike her roomates who spent their money on ski trips or trips to exotic places, which costs a bundle, even with the perks of working for an airline. They bought expensive gifts for men and their families, cheap clothes by the closet full and cheap makeup.

Emily, on the other hand, carefully selected everything she bought. From her underwear to her lipstick, it was a meticulous selection process, and it showed. She was wise way beyond her upbringing and years.

It wouldn't be long before her investments would be very large and she could live wherever she wanted. She put most of her salary into her portfolio, which had far surpassed even Emily's wildest expectations.


SHE BEGAN PACING THE SMALL room, waiting for the driver's call to say he was on his way. She haphazardly picked up one of the dozens of brochures lying on the table and began leafing through the points of interest for the tenth time, marking and remarking places she wanted to visit. It had taken her hours last night to decide the tour route. Eric would probably like museums and cultural stops, she had guessed— places Emily had not had the time to visit. But, he would never know that. She had gone to the library at 7 o'clock and checked out every book on Seattle she could find. Within 24 hours Emily felt like an expert on the subject. If she was out to impress anyone, this was one time she would not fail. Not that Emily felt like she was going to fail. She wasn't sure how she felt, but she did know that she had never felt this way before.

She checked her reflection one more time. The pale yellow skirt and sweater set she had purchased at Bergdorf Goodman on a recent trip to New York was perfect. The collar was trimmed with tiny intricately embroidered mint green leaves and rosebuds. The a-line skirt hugged her trim figure. The telephone rang as Emily tucked a loose hair back into place. She picked up the receiver gingerly and took a deep breath, because she knew in her heart that this man was getting ready to change her life forever.

ERIC PROVED HE KNEW HOW to treat a woman. When Emily emerged from her apartment complex a young man in a chauffeur's uniform jumped from the car to assist her. The rush of excitement coursed through her body. She was a little girl playing princess for a day. Already she didn't want the day to end, and it had just begun.

Once inside the elegant car, she inhaled deeply, taking in the rich aroma of fine leather. She leaned against the cool seats, trying to calm her quivering stomach.  As the car deftly made its way through the city in which she was to play tour guide, Emily's confidence grew. She knew what she wanted. Now, all she had to do was get it.

ERIC STOOD OUTSIDE THE BEAUTIFUL OLYMPIC Hotel. It didn't surprise Emily that Eric would select and stay at the city's premier luxury hotel. Since it was built in 1924, its charm and beauty had never faded. She studied the man standing there, waiting for her. She soaked in every detail of his starched shirt, the beautiful pale blue cashmere sweater tied loosely around his neck, the gabardine slacks with a slight crisp pressed edge, his hand casually tucked in his pocket, the other, holding a beautiful spray of daisies. The complete portrait of a successful man. The perfect picture of a man, Emily thought.

Emily wondered if a man could be a vision of loveliness as she watched him stride toward the car.  His eyes sparkled and Emily began to melt.  As he opened the door and eased himself in next to her, she could smell his sweet scent. If Eric Blake was anything at all, he was all man.

"Good morning, beautiful lady. First, I want to apologize for not being in the car when Charles picked you up this morning. I had a business call that could not be avoided. But I am now one hundred percent yours and am ready to be ooed and aahed all day with your terrific tour," he teased, as he gently brushed his lips against her cheek. In her best business tone, Emily replied in jest, "Well, my dear Mister Blake, you have a full day of activities arranged for you. Please sit back and leave the touring to the professionals."

Both giggled, sounding like young children exploring each other for the first time, sniffing each other out to see if the boy likes the girl or the girl likes the boy.

The first stop on the tour was Alki Point Lighthouse. The tidy little lighthouse had been built in 1913 and was situated above a pebbled beach overlooking Puget Sound at the southern entrance to Elliot Bay. It was close to the city, and Emily thought it was good place to start. From there the pair headed to West Point Lighthouse. The lighthouse sat at the end of a low sandy point that extended out into Puget Sound. At one time it served as a marker to the entrance of the water link between Puget Sound, Lake Union, and Lake Washington. Emily loved watching the alternating red and white flashes of light emitting from its beacon.

After the lighthouses, Emily thought it might be fun to check out the Space Needle, which had been constructed for the 1962 World's Fair. The top of the Needle offered an expansive view of all of the surrounding area, and, today, Mount Rainier was clearly visible. It appeared to be no farther than one hundred yards away, when in reality it was one hundred miles to the southeast of the city.

Emily's stomach was rumbling so she knew her lunch plans were playing in with her schedule perfectly. Emily instructed the driver to head to the Central Waterfront area and the old piers 54 and 55. Emily had made reservations at Ivar's Acres of Clams, a must stop for every seafood lover, and a fun stop to boot.

Emily ordered her favorite dish of steamed clams and fresh tomatoes and cucumber salad. Eric took over just long enough to order an exquisite bottle of a crisp dry chardonnay. The twosome leisurely lunched and chatted about their next stop, which was the Marine Aquarium just around the corner. It was just a few years old and at the end of Pier 56. She was excited to see the display of killer whales. As she described the orcas and the aquarium's famous resident Namu, Eric found himself laughing and smiling and bemused by this woman child. He was having a good time and he liked it.

As the tour slowly wound down, Emily was very pleased. She almost convinced herself that she had done the tour hundreds of times and had been to every museum at least three times. Eric didn't miss a beat. He was as impressed with Emily as Emily was with herself. They were exhausted yet happy and relaxed with one another as the car edged to the curb of Emily's apartment complex, signaling the end of a wonderful day.

Eric leaned over, stopping her hand from touching the door. "Not yet. You don't think I could just have you give me the A plus tour of the century and just drop you off like a common tour guide, do you? No my dear. I must repay your kindness," Eric said, placing his hand over his heart. "I insist I take you to the finest restaurant in the city and wine and dine you to your heart's content. Please tell me you have no other tours to give this evening so this young man will not be heartbroken."

Emily burst into laughter at his silliness. She beamed up at him, yet kept her cool as always, and said, "Yes, Mister Blake, you may repay my kindness and, in lieu of payment for the tour, dinner is quite acceptable by my company."

The two shared a laugh then locked eyes. It was Eric who finally broke the silence. "Shall I pick you up at eight?" Emily only nodded until she could find her voice again, and when she did speak, it was soft and quiet. "Eight would be just perfect."

# Chapter Four

THE NEXT TWO MONTHS WERE a whirlwind of activity for Emily. Her flights took her to Portland every other day, if not everyday some weeks. She flew to Chicago twice and even to Atlanta once. Three times her schedule had indicated layovers in Atlanta with quick trips to Charlotte. She wasn't a fool. Paul Brady was playing with her schedule. She played the game back and had switched flights with another girl.

The only thing she wanted to do was get back to Seattle and to Eric. He consumed her. Her thoughts, her wishes, and her desires all centered around him. Yet, she didn't even know where he was from. Did he have brothers or sisters? Were his parents alive? What college had he attended? She often thought of asking him about his life, but somewhere in the recesses of her mind, she knew not to.

She didn't know if she was afraid to find out he was married and only able to see her on her scheduled days off, or if he had other women. Whenever she steered the conversation into personal territory, Eric had the uncanny ability to turn the subject to another. The maneuver didn't escape Emily's attention. She had mastered the move herself.

She did know that he had money and wasn't afraid to spend it on her and the evenings they enjoyed together. Eric always bought the best wines. The restaurants were the finest in the city. He knew how to order and speak the language. Nothing intimidated Eric. He traveled as much and as often as she, calling her from cities across the country and the seas. She had never been so happy. She felt she now knew the true meaning of love, because she was in it.

❧ ✳ ❧

As soon as the plane touched down, Emily hurried the passengers off. "Don't forget your wrap, Madame."

"Oh, thank you dear. Why if I had left that I..." Emily cut her off, ushering her forward.

"Yes, well fortunately I saw it. Let's just put it on."

Emily was on a mission. Eric only had two days in town and she didn't want to waste a second talking to passengers. Her co-workers laughed at her little girl antics.

"Emily, slow down. You can't push them out the door," they teased.

Emily rolled her eyes as she continued to herd everyone down the aisles. For all of her almost 22 years, Emily had looked for someone to just love her. She believed she had found that someone in Eric. He had never pressured her to make love. "You'll know when the time is right, Emily," he had gently whispered into her ear.

"So, can you trade schedules with me tomorrow or not, Emily?" The dark haired stewardess asked Emily again.

Emily stared at her.

"Please Emily. I'll kick in a little something extra."

Emily shook her head as she finally realized she was being spoken to, and laughed. "I couldn't trade with you for all the money in the world." And she meant it. She had decided that tonight was the right night. She had not given herself to the one person in the world she wanted to please the most. And now the time had come.

"Eric was right," she said to herself. "I did know when the time was right." She thought of those lonely nights and shuddered. She wasn't going to risk losing Eric. She wasn't a virgin, but she wasn't one because of her own doing. "Don't think about that now," she chided herself. "Just keep moving forward as far away from that life as possible."

Emily wanted to replace her past with new cites, a new family, and a new childhood. She had told Eric early in their relationship that she was from a small town in Kentucky, and that most of her family was dead. She couldn't tell him she had been lying. No, if Eric loved her, he would just have to believe her. There was no one but her in the world. Emily almost believed it herself.

She raced out of the terminal and hailed a cab. The constant drizzle snarled traffic, making her nervous and leaving her on edge. She had a million things to do before she saw Eric—or before Eric saw her. Emily's strict regimen was followed, no matter the delays. She had to have a manicure, her hair washed and set, a fragrant bath, and her clothes perfectly cleaned and ironed. It didn't bother her if they didn't eat until eleven. She would do everything to make herself perfect before he could see her. Emily knew the affect she had on Eric. She took his breath away. She was going to make sure that never changed.

Jumping from the cab, Emily hurried inside her apartment. The telephone was already ringing. It had taken a record breaking slow speed of one hour to get from the terminal to her front door. She was behind schedule. "Damn. Slow down Emily. Catch your breath," she said. Taking a deep breath and praying it was Eric, Emily slowly picked up the receiver. "Hello."

Paul Brady's voice crawled through the line, "Hello Pumpkin. Glad I caught you at home. I've been watching your schedule. You've changed that little Charlotte trip three times on old Paul. You don't ever call your old buddy, either. What's the deal? Don't you like the boss anymore?"

Emily's heart was racing and her palms were sweating. "Think, Emily. Think." Her mind screamed at her. She didn't trust her own voice and thought she would choke if words tried to escape. She shuddered at the sound of his voice. She could almost imagine a snake curling itself around her, squeezing the very life from her.

Oh, she had known sooner or later it would come to this. He had gotten her the plum assignment available at the time. Working first class on direct routes could have taken her almost two years. Paul had done it immediately. Now, here he was on the other end of the line, tying it up, wanting to chit chat. The only thing she wanted to do was slam the receiver down or shout that she was waiting for Eric to call and her line couldn't be busy. But, instead she spoke sweetly.

"Why, hello Paul. How are you?" she purred.

"Well, I'd be a whole lot better if I could finally have me a little dose of you. I sure have missed you," he said, trying to sound hurt.

Emily felt her stomach muscles tighten. Steadying herself against the small foyer table, she continued in her pleasant tone. "That may just be impossible. I'm not scheduled to come to Charlotte for some time now, and I've been really busy. Every day I have off I usually spend at home with my family, or they come here."

She knew as soon as the words were out of her mouth that she had made a mistake. She knew he knew she was lying. He could just check her freebie record.

"Damn, now what?" Emily scolded herself. Paul cleared his throat. She could hear him shuffling through papers on his desk. When he spoke, his voice was clear and unmistakable.

"I've put in a special request for you. I guess you're coming to Charlotte sooner than you thought. Now, you be sure to be on the Charlotte leg. Don't be giving it away. I really want to see you. You know, for old time's sake? So, you just check your pretty little self into the Airport Hotel like a good little girl, then I will come and visit. You understand, don't you?"

Emily clutched the telephone until her knuckles were white. Her mind was reeling. She didn't hear much more of the conversation. Nor did she have to. She started to tell him she had met someone and had fallen in love. That she would never let another man touch her. But, she knew she would be losing her job.

"Sure Paul. I'll do that. I look forward to seeing you."

"That's good, Em. Real good. I can't wait to slip in to see you," he chuckled nastily. "You take care of yourself, Em, till Boss Paul takes care of ya."

Emily stared at the telephone in disbelief as the line went dead. Slowly she edged her way to the couch and sank deep into its cushions. Lowering her head into her hands, she began to sob.

Maybe if she told Eric he would understand and help her. Never, Emily thought. Eric will never know about any of this. As the sun began to set, darkness filled the room. Emily sat still in the silence. Slowly, she rose and went to the bathroom to fill the tub with warm water and sweet smelling scents. She lit candles and let the soft orange glow cast shadows across the small room. A plan was forming in her head. A smile started to tug at the corners of her mouth, and finally a full grin crept across her lips. Yes, she could handle the likes of a Paul Brady. Just one more obstacle in her way.  And Emily wasn't about to let any obstacle get in her way.

# Chapter Five

ERIC LEANED AGAINST THE BEDPOST in his hotel room. He'd had a terrible week. His business dealings had gone bad over the past few days. The women he had seen in other cities hadn't satisfied him. He was tired of playing the games. He knew he had to make some changes and make them fast.

Eric lived a very rich life and his resources were running thin. If he didn't find some new investments, he would find himself in trouble. Of course, all it took was one big score. He got up and mixed himself a stiff gin and tonic.

"Yeah, that's all I need," he mused. "Just one big score and I'm back on top. Nobody will screw with me then. Calling my margins, calling my debts, calling my ass on the carpet. I work damn hard."

Eric continued his tirade as he began to pace about the elegant suite. He tossed the drink back, savoring its bitter taste. Wiping his mouth with his hand, he felt better. He picked up the telephone. "I know one person who always makes me feel better."

As soon as he heard Emily's voice, his own voice softened, as did his mood. "I knew if I could just hear your voice, my world would be all right. How quickly can you be ready? And don't say three hours, because I can't and won't wait three hours, Emily. I must see you."

His pleas sounded urgent, but Emily remained constant and strong. "Eric, I would love to dash out of this door this instant and fall into your arms, but I just this second got off of an airplane after six days in the air and I must get organized. You'll have to be a true sweetheart and give me at least two hours. Please?"

Emily was met with silence on the other end. Finally he broke the quiet and with great calm simply said, "How can you do this to me? Anyone else and I would say forget it. But with you, it is always yes. I will see you in two hours. But Emily, please do not be late. I have something very special in mind for us tonight."

Emily felt her body shudder with excitement. "Eric, I won't be late."

She replaced the receiver and stared at the telephone. Her heart was pounding. There was something about his voice. It was smooth, yet chilling. "How could he have known I was ready to give myself to him?"

Then chiding herself, "Oh, don't be so dramatic, Emily. Maybe it's a new restaurant or a new wine or a new something. He probably wants you to be his wife, that's all. No big deal. Just, 'Emily, I can't live without you. I am miserable. Quit this flying around and come be with me forever.' "

Emily stopped and studied her reflection in the mirror. She started to laugh. Her face was glowing. "Funny, Emily. Very funny."

ERIC STROLLED INTO THE HOTEL lobby. Glancing about, he had to admire the beautiful surroundings with its splendid old world charm of Italian renaissance architecture. He stopped to admire the enormous ornate flower arrangements in crystal vases adorning each of the large pink marbled tables. The flowers ranged from exotic bird of paradise to pink lilies to deep purple orchids flown in fresh from the Hawaiian Islands. Their sweet fragrance filled the air. The Olympic Hotel had opened in the midst of the roaring '20s with a dinner and dance on December 6, 1924. It was a milestone for the Pacific Northwest that something this beautiful and spectacular was now a part of Seattle's history. More than 2,000 people had attended the gala affair and hundreds had lined the streets in hopes of catching a glimpse of the glamour and beauty on the inside. Eric started to feel better. He looked at the inlaid marble tiled floor and the rich oak paneling with its carved designs.

There were many beautiful hotels and homes and places Eric had visited and seen, but this was one of his favorite. He didn't know if it were the surroundings and the decor he loved so much or the fact that he always associated it with Emily.

Checking his watch, he felt the edginess begin to creep back in again. He might have time to make another quick trip to the room, but he didn't want to chance it. No. He could wait.

Emily would be his fix. He knew she would. She always was. Eric turned and tugged on his gold cufflinks to tighten them. He heard the soft and demure sound of someone clearing their throat to get attention. As he slowly turned, he saw her standing there.

Beautiful in a red beaded gown, slit to expose her long slender legs, her hair cascading down her back, Emily just stood there quietly. He leaned in close to her, softly kissing her lips, taking in the sweet scent of tropical flowers. He took his forefinger and gently traced it down her bare back and down her soft arms.

"My God. You take my breath away," he whispered. "I would hate to have been the poor soul you kept waiting had you had another hour to get ready."

Emily almost purred. "You always know just the right thing to say to a woman, and it's good to see you too, Prince Charming."

Eric touched her elbow and guided her to the waiting car. Once inside, he soaked in her beauty. "You are the most gorgeous creature. I am completely at your service, but you probably already know that, huh?"

Emily just smiled. She liked the sense of power she had over him. She could be thirty minutes late and still he was never angry with her.

She said not a word. She knew when she had walked into the hotel lobby that he was tense. She had studied him while his back was facing her. She had seen him checking his watch. She was fifteen minutes late and he had asked her to be on time. But Emily, like Eric, liked to do things her way.

As soon as their eyes met, time and all of the other unnecessary elements of the when and what had faded into nothingness. For the first time in the relationship, Emily felt electricity so strong she almost wanted to bolt.

But she didn't bolt. Instead, she listened in awe as Eric described his international business dealings from the past two weeks.

"So, here I am in the middle of Paris and this man is speaking French so fast that all I can do is wave my hands in the air. 'Monsieur, me parlent lentement,' I say trying my best to get him to speak to me slowly. But, he keeps rattling on. I think he's the big shot I am to meet with, and I'm wondering where the hell the interpreter is. All of a sudden, out of nowhere comes this little old lady, who grabs the man by the ear and just carts him off. Just like that, he is gone. I'm standing there, and the real Monsieur Beluga comes up and, in perfect English, apologizes for being late. Incredible."

Emily wiped the tears of laughter from her face. Through fits of giggles, she managed to ask a question.

"How on earth do you get yourself into messes like that? What did you say to him?"

Pretending to be shocked, Eric continued his story.

"Say to him? I said nothing! I had been conversing with the resident florist, and I had taken a flower for my lapel. Not a smart thing to do. He was, let's just say, extremely angry with me. The woman happened to run the hotel and was coming to my rescue."

Emily couldn't remember when she had laughed so hard. Every detail of Eric's life was full of excitement. The travel, the stories, and the people he met. Eric was everything she had ever dreamed of, and he was making her past truly disappear for her.

That is all she had ever really wanted in her life. Watching her intensely, Eric said, "And what, my pretty, is going through that beautiful little head of yours?" Blushing at having been caught, Emily simply stated, "Here I have these investments. I think I'm so smart and doing so well. Then I look at you. I'm proud of you. You are going through my head."

Eric gingerly touched her hand. "As far as your investments go, I have looked at them for you and you are doing very well. I am proud of you." He squeezed her hand tightly. The small hairs on her arms rose at his touch.

"And you are going through every other fiber of my body," she replied honestly.

Eric regarded her closely. He tenderly picked up her hands, turning them ever so slowly in his. "Are you sure?" he asked.

"Oh, yes. I am very sure," Emily whispered.

EMILY STOOD IN THE MIDDLE of the elegant suite, surrounded by flowers and champagne. The walls were covered in a gold embossed cloth; the curtains were heavy gold velvet. The carpet was thick and plush and cushioned. She felt as if she were walking on clouds.

Eric dimmed the lights and soft soothing music filled the air. Emily knew she had made the right decision. Eric approached her slowly, encircling her in his arms, and he said, "Do not be frightened or afraid. I know in my heart this was meant to be."

"I'm not afraid and I want this. More than anything, I want this."

Eric turned her to face him. With expert hands and skill he unbuttoned each of the red encrusted beaded buttons revealing her swollen breasts. Emily wondered if she was going to faint. She had never really made love to a man. Men had only used her body. Her mind, her soul, and her heart had never been there. But tonight, every nerve in her body was on fire. She felt her breath quicken under his touch.

Eric was sure she was a virgin. This is exactly what he wanted. He took his fingers and outlined her breast, and then moved on to touch her nipple as it hardened to his touch. Tenderly and without a word spoken between them, he slipped the red gown from her hips and let it fall silently to the floor.

Emily stood very still, almost naked, in the middle of the room. She was having trouble breathing. Could Eric hear the pounding of her heart?

He reached up and stroked her neck, letting his fingers tug through her hair, lifting the golden mane from her shoulders and pulling it back away from her face. He wanted to look at her. She was his goddess.

Emily felt like a goddess. Ever so slowly, Eric kissed her neck and made his way to her breasts, where his tongue licked at the hard nipples, causing her to groan in pleasure. Emily tried to steady herself by grabbing his shoulder. He pushed her hand away.

"Stand just like that. Very still my love." Eric continued licking her breast, and then cupped them tenderly in his hands. He knelt before her, sliding his tongue down her flat stomach. Emily had never known sensations such as this existed. The force of his touch was overwhelming. She bit into her lip to remain standing.

"Please, I can't stand…"

"Right where you are, don't move," Eric said deeply.

"Now, remove your stockings while I watch, and do so very slowly."

Emily did as she was told, unsnapping the hook of each garter belt, slowly curling the hosiery downward and slipping each off her feet. Finally, Eric took her in his arms and lifted her in the air. Emily couldn't breathe. She was more alive than she ever thought she could be. She was in love and, for the first time in her life, she was going to make love to the man she loved.

Eric gently laid her on the large bed. The cool satin sheets felt good against her skin. Emily closed her eyes and let him take her away. Away from her past. Away from the terrible ghosts that haunted her. Away from herself. Away from the world. If anything was wrong, Emily certainly didn't feel it or see it.

# Chapter Six

EMILY FLEW INTO CHARLOTTE as scheduled. She gathered her belongings from the small overhead compartment and looked at her friend Susan.

"Hey, Susan. I'm getting an incredible migraine. I think I'll skip dinner with you tonight. If I don't get to feeling better, do you think we could switch schedules for a few days? That way I could pack it on out of here first thing in the morning and head home."

Susan didn't wait to jump on the offer. Of course, Emily knew she wouldn't refuse. Emily knew Susan had the hots for the pilot of the plane, and anytime she could stay an extra few days with him were just fine with her.

"Not a problem. Don't worry about dinner, I sort of wanted to stay in myself, if you know what I mean," Susan winked.

"Thanks, I owe you one." Emily smiled, thinking how transparent her friend really was. Susan would have paid her to switch schedules. With a determined step, Emily exited the plane and headed for her next destination.

She knew she had a lot of work to do in a very short period of time. Her heart was racing. "God, this is almost exciting," she chuckled. Her plan had to work. If it didn't, she was out of a job and probably out of a relationship.

Eric would know everything about her and she would probably have to rely on her savings and investments until she could find another job. And if good old Paul was right about his power, then finding another job may take a long time, she thought. She wouldn't get a referral. She would be signing her own death warrant.

Hurriedly, she checked into her hotel room. She took a bath and lit candles and changed into a soft lightweight, comfortable nightgown. She flipped through the room service offerings before dialing hotel guest services.

"Please send two bottles of Dom Perignon to room 727, please...Yes. Just put it on my room charge." With the order completed, Emily lay down on the bed, folded her hands under her head, and smiled as she looked at the clock and waited.


PAUL BRADY PULLED INTO THE hotel parking lot. Glancing around the lot, he drove straight to the "Employees Only" parking spaces. There was no way he was going to pay to park. He gave this hotel too much money, he reasoned. Plus, he was a big shot here. He straightened his tie, slapped some aftershave on his cheeks, and took a big swig of mouthwash, swishing it around before spitting it onto the asphalt.

As he entered the hotel lobby, Paul looked around for any familiar faces. The young bellboy immediately jumped to his aid, and said, "Good evening, Mr. Brady. May I help you?"

Slipping the boy a one dollar bill, he swaggered up to him. "Yeah, the usual."

The boy took the single bill and slid it into his pocket, smiling. "You got it Mr. B. You got it."

As Paul Brady strutted toward the bank of elevators, the boy shook his head and went directly to the wall of house telephones. Quickly dialing, he spoke quietly into the receiver. "He's on his way up," is all he said before hanging the phone up.

A loud laugh escaped his lips. "And that, sir, is for being such a cheap son of a bitch. At least the lady knows how to tip," he said, as he got out a crisp twenty dollar bill and kissed it.

As Paul Brady got off the elevator, he danced a little hip hop down the hall. Whistling a forgotten tune, he was in the best of spirits. Why shouldn't he be? Emily Anderson was going to be the best piece of ass he had ever had in his life. And she was crazy for him. He had so many young girls from the airline in and out of this hotel he thought they should rename the place the "Hotel Paul Brady Stud Puppy." He laughed heartily at himself.

He slicked his hair back into place and cupped his hand over his mouth to smell his breath. He had to hand it to the little lady. She had gotten the right room. Room number 727. Only a smart one like Emily would think of that.

Her skin is so soft, he thought, feeling his erection grow. Too bad he only had an hour to spend with her. His wife was at a church meeting and would be home early tonight. Damn, bad timing on his part, he thought. He should have told her something earlier in the week. But, how was he to know she was going to cancel her weekly bridge club meeting for a church meeting? "Oh well, as hot as Emily is, I can get a lot of action in one short hour," he mused.

Feeling proud as a peacock, Paul looked down at his swollen member. He felt like a young boy. Coming to room 727, he cleared his throat and knocked on the door, "Excuse me. Room service has arrived, and I do mean service."

The door swung open and a beautiful young woman stood there. She was petite, but her breasts were bursting to the point where they overflowed from the pale sheer yellow negligee. Her luxurious red hair fell past her shoulders. Paul looked at her small feet, which were in high heel slip-ons. Even the puffy balls were yellow and matched her negligee.

"Hi. I'm Beth. Emily's running a little late, so she said for me to entertain you for a few minutes. We have champagne on ice. The works."

Looking down at Paul's crotch, Beth sighed, "Oh, baby. It looks like Emily is really going to get it tonight."

Paul Brady didn't quite know what to do. But he managed a smile.

"A twosome? I never really figured Em for the type, but what the hell. While I'm waiting, I've got a little something for you. Get down on this, whore."

As Paul roughly grabbed Beth's head and shoved her to the floor, he unzipped his pants to reveal his erection. As he pranced into the room, holding Beth by the hair, she let out a shriek of pain.

"Oh, come on bitch. You love it, or you wouldn't be here. Now put this in your mouth and it'll keep you quiet for a minute." Paul threw his head back and then heard another person clear their throat. His eyes flew open and he stopped dead in his tracks.

Seated on the small sofa and two side chairs were his wife and two women from their church. He recognized both of them immediately. Evelyn Turner and her husband headed up the social events for their country club. Faye Palmer's husband, Fred, was Paul's loan officer at the bank. His social status and his financial status stared back at him. Plus, there was his wife.

She sat upright, with a tissue held to her nose. Rosemary Brady was a plumb woman of 40 years. She was neatly dressed, holding a folder and pen in her hand. Slowly, she rose from her seat and lowered the material to the sofa.

Looking at Paul with eyes filled first with hatred, and then with tears of sorrow and sadness and betrayal, she maintained her composure.

"Paul, I didn't want to believe the young woman who called me today, saying you held special prayer meetings here at the hotel. I thought it was some kind of joke. She gave me her name and several others. She left some photographs here for me tonight. She asked that I keep them for my own personal use. I haven't looked at them, Paul, but she did say if she were to lose her job, she had more to send to the company's president."

With that said Rosemary turned to her two friends and motioned for them to leave. All three walked silently out of the room and gently closed the door.

Paul turned, his limp friend still hanging from his unzipped pants.

Beth grabbed her coat, and said, "That was definitely worth a hundred dollars. See ya around sometime, Paul. Oh, and Emily wanted me to tell you there's only been one person on this earth that ever called her Em, and that person is not you. So don't ever address her that way again. See ya!"

Paul Brady looked around the empty room. Slowly, he put his pitiful friend back into his pants and zipped up. Glancing about, he saw an envelope with his name on it. With a growing unease, he picked it up and opened it. A single sheet of paper with several women's names appeared on it. He knew them all well. Too well. No doubt about it. Emily had done her homework, and done it well. And he knew there was nothing he could do about it.


"CAN I GET YOU ANYTHING ELSE to drink, sir?" Emily asked the gentleman in the front aisle of the first class section. She glanced down at her watch and smiled. "This is truly a very special evening, sir. How about some champagne?"

Emily was euphoric as the plane sped toward Seattle. Within four hours she would be in her own bed. Too bad Eric thought she would be out of town and would not call. If he didn't travel so much she could get a number from him to call. But Eric was a lot like her. She lived in the air and he lived on the land, going from city to city, with home being just somewhere to hang your hat. But things were moving so fast between them that Emily felt in her heart that their relationship was destined to change. And change fast.

# Chapter Seven

THE RINGING TELEPHONE SHATTERED the silence in Emily's deathly quiet apartment. Her pulse quickened as she hurried to answer the taunting machine. She knew Eric's husky voice was just seconds away from her. She glanced at the wall clock. Almost six o'clock. She had been listening to each second tick away before the telephone had finally rung.

Her high heels clipped the top of the thick green shag carpet, almost causing her to trip. Slow down, Emily thought. She would never let Eric know she had not left the apartment all day because she was waiting for his call. She had paid the extra money to have a hairdresser come to her, as well as a manicurist. She firmly believed the extra expense was worth it. Besides, her stock broker had done wonders for her investments in the past year.

She had dined with him just last week. He was very pleased with himself for having turned a modest investment portfolio into a substantial amount of money. Although Emily could tell he would like to be appreciated more and in a more personal way, she wasn't the least bit interested or intimidated. She was a business client just like anyone else. But an occasional long look and slow sexy smile and lick of her lips around him never hurt. So she had let him kiss her once. Just once. At least this way she knew her investments would continue to grow.

If he thought he had the slightest of chances of getting her under the sheets, he was going to make sure her profit sheet continued to increase. Emily kept him at a distance, yet not too far away. She actually liked him, and if Eric had never entered the picture, maybe their friendship could have blossomed into something more. But that was not the case. Eric had entered the picture, and in a big way.

She didn't want to get an apartment all to herself. Not just yet. She truly felt that she and Eric were moving toward marriage.

Even though their time together had been limited in the past few months, due to his extensive travel, she knew it was only a matter of time before she would become Mrs. Eric Blake. That's really all that kept her going these days. She scoffed at that idea.

"Let a man take over my life. Ha! That will be the day!" But even as she said it aloud, she knew it was true. He had totally consumed her. He went over her investments with her. He guided her on where to put her money. He helped her buy clothes. He sent her small but elegant gifts. In nine months time, Eric had taught her some French, how to taste and recognize and order fine wines, know real gems from fake ones, and how to possess more confidence than she had ever known she could— except when she was with him. With him, Emily became childlike, depending on him for every direction.

And that is just how he liked it. Emily assumed Eric needed her to need him. And she did need him. And she wanted him. The telephone continued to ring. She let it ring three times before finally snatching it up. Calmly, and self assured, she answered.

"Hello? Oh, hi sweetheart. I just got back from the hairdresser. Seven would be lovely."

Eric smiled into the receiver. He could see her in his mind, sitting, then standing, pacing, dancing as the telephone had rung. She didn't fool him. No one fooled Eric Blake. But he didn't care. He needed and even wanted Emily Anderson. And tonight, he was going to make sure she was his.


EMILY SMOOTHED THE IMAGINARY wrinkles from her dress and took one more deep relaxing breath. She knocked on the door of the elegant hotel suite just before eight o'clock sharp. Eric slowly opened the door, and then in one swift fluid motion, he swept her into his arms, causing her to gasp for breath before being consumed with laughter at his antics.

"My goodness, one would think I had been missed."

"Missed, my darling is not the word," he mused. "More like pined for."

Emily drank in his words as she felt his firm grip around her waist. With him, nothing could go wrong. He was her knight in shining armor. He was everything she had ever wanted in a man.

Eric held her tight. "You look good enough to eat. Are you sure you want to leave and have dinner?"

Emily threw her head back in ecstasy. "I would starve to death before I would miss a chance to make love to you."

Eric slowly began to undress her. As his fingers moved up and down her body, knowing every curve, every bone, he slid her panties to the floor and lifted her to him, propelling them both to the bed. Emily closed her eyes and let a smile cross her face. It was always here, in Eric's arms, in his loving embrace, that she felt she was safe and free from harm. Eric's hunger for her overwhelmed her. He was fast and furious. His lovemaking was strong and brilliant, bringing them both to a quick and glorious and much anticipated climax. As they lay in one another's arms, Eric gently touched her hair. "Would you prefer room service tonight?" he asked. "Yes, that would be lovely," she said, stretching her long limbs before him. He picked up the telephone and called room service.

"Yes, I would like Chateaubriand pour deux, plus bring extra au jus, a 1957 bottle of Rothschild, and a bottle of your best champagne…Oui. Merci."

Eric turned to her and soaked in her raw beauty. She sensed a change in him and held her breath. She didn't know what to expect. She wasn't scared. She honestly didn't know what she was because this sensation had never been felt. Timidly, she pulled the satin sheet around her bare breasts. Eric reached over and pulled the fabric away from her.

"This isn't how I expected tonight to be. I thought we would be having a romantic evening high above Seattle in the revolving restaurant of the Space Needle. You know, return to one of the very first places you took me on my tour. In fact, they are probably wondering where we are right about now. But, such is life." Eric rose and stood naked before her. A devilish smile curled across his sensuous lips. He slowly knelt to one knee. "My dear and beautiful Emily, will you please marry me?"

Emily was awestruck. She had not expected the expected. Not tonight. Not here. Not like this. She heard herself suck in extra breath, finding it difficult to breathe. All of her dreams were coming true. It was really happening. She was going to be the woman she wanted to be, Mrs. Eric Blake.

"I am naked in bed with you, so this proposal might be a little difficult to tell our children about, so we'll have to stick with your original plan as to when you did the asking. But, yes, Eric, I will marry you. I love you more than anything in the world, and I want to spend my life with you."

Emily let the tears stream down her face, causing her massacre to run a little. For once, she didn't even care. Eric held her tightly, thinking he had never said anything about children. She clung to him, thinking most women would want to call someone they loved to share such news. She had no one to call. But now, she had someone to love. She had Eric.

# Chapter Eight

THE OLD WAREHOUSE STOOD alone. It had been used during World War II as a mechanic's shop for repairing old parts for reuse. The all wood structure was now the possession of the Port of Seattle, which planned to raze most of the buildings in the area. During a bygone era, the latest tunes would have been heard blaring from a radio, filling the night air. Those who listened would have been filled with high spirits. Those who had returned from the war had continued to do their duty, and those who were unable to fight, had found solace here, helping the war effort.

But today, the warehouse was chillingly quiet. A cold breeze rattled its broken windows. The tin covered rusting roof shook and gave way in several places under the upcoming storm's power. A stretch limousine pulled up to the front of the warehouse, looking oddly out of place. Two dark suited, burly, black haired men bounced from the car. At first, they just scanned the area, looking from side to side. Then, signaling each other, they moved to the back of the long sleek vehicle, both attentive to their surroundings. Their eyes continued to dart back and forth.

A frail elderly man emerged, wrapped in a charcoal gray cashmere overcoat and matching fedora. His shoes were of soft Italian leather. He motioned for the two bulking assistants to open the warehouse door just by flicking his forefinger in its direction, never uttering a word.

The heavy, rickety sliding doors didn't give easily. Brandishing guns, the men entered first, leaving the old man unattended for a minute. He stood, eyes closed, as if meditating, calmly letting the cold winter wind whirl around him. Having cleared his entrance, the two men escorted him into the warehouse. Inside was a different story.

The building had small electrical heaters running throughout. Square tables were set up, as well as a long conference table. File folders and cabinets filled the once empty space. Hot coffee brewed and the thick bittersweet aroma filled the air. The old man was led to the head of the table. Men appeared from the recesses of the warehouse to take his coat and hat, bring coffee, and files.

From the back of the warehouse, Eric watched the proceedings in fascination. He wondered how long it had taken the old man to arrive at such power. That was the kind of power Eric longed for. He had dreaded this meeting and had actually been able to put it off for a week by claiming he was having trouble finalizing the deal. One week was all the old man had given him. He could have given him ten weeks and Eric still wouldn't have the deal put together. He knew that. Now he was afraid the old man knew it too.

Eric gathered his courage and strode from the back room, trying to look as confident as possible. He stared squarely into old but wise pale blue eyes. They were slightly red rimmed and watered from age. Their color had lost their brilliancy years ago, but they were still strong and unflinching. They showed no emotion, but Eric knew from one glance that they held so much power. So much knowledge.

"Good afternoon, Sir. I trust your trip here went well." In an uncharacteristically clear and deep voice, the old man spoke. "Yes Eric. The trip went well. But this trip should be unnecessary for me, as you know. Now, come sit with me and let us talk over the problems we seem to be having."

Eric moved cautiously, watching the hovering assistants. He tried to position himself so that his back would be against the only wall in the building. But he knew if anyone wanted to kill him, he was outnumbered, outmaneuvered, and out of luck. Eric slumped in his seat. "Sir, I can explain," Eric started.

The old man raised his bony hand to cut him off. "No Eric. I will explain. We gave you a large sum of money to buy certain products and you have not produced the products. Now, you can either give me my money back with interest, or give me my merchandise. It is really very simple. You have accomplished this in the past. Why you ran into a problem I do not know. I do not want explanations. I do not work well with explanations.

"Now if someone has stolen from you then that is a different story. Then we find that someone and they will tell us the truth. Or perhaps you did not work correctly and you were detained by the authorities. But if that were the case, you would not be here right now. Eric, I have much tied up in this particular project. You are one of the keys to the entire operation. Please do not make me change the lock. Do I make myself clear?"

Eric stilled himself. "I have most of your money, sir. I can have the rest of it for you by week's end. Our contacts are running scared. The authorities are just too close for comfort. I cannot obtain closure."

The old man studied Eric closely for a minute before speaking. "I cannot understand why you do not have the money with you now. All of it. I should kill you. I should watch you die. But for the family's sake, I will spare your pathetic little life. I will be watching you, Eric. You may buy some time and when I am ready I will see you. Time is money, so you will be notified. But, if I am not satisfied when that time comes, you will die a slow and painful death. Is that clear?"

Keeping his eyes trained on the old man, Eric nodded. "Yes Sir. Very clear." Eric tried to keep his voice strong. He could feel his knees begin to shake. He cleared his throat to speak again, but the old man was finished.

Dismissively, he waved his feeble hand. Eric rose and looked at him almost pleadingly, but he would not return his stare.

"More coffee here, Bino." As far as the old man was concerned, Eric had already left the room.

Eric turned on his heels and retreated to the rear of the warehouse. He got into his car and revved its engine. He sat there trying to warm his hands as the ailing heater refused to emit heat. Suddenly, he slammed his hand against the dashboard. "Damn it! How in the hell am I going to come up with ten grand?"

Reaching into the glove compartment, he fingered a gun, turning it back and forth for a moment before resting it beside him on the front seat. Then he reached in and pulled out a sheet of white school paper folded into a square. It resembled a child's note one would pass around the classroom with its edges folded over and tucked into one another.

Eric carefully unfolded the note. But there was no writing on the paper. Instead, a white powder filled the square. Taking a one dollar bill, he rolled it tightly, fashioning it into the shape of an extra thin straw. Sticking the homemade straw into his nostril, Eric inhaled deeply, sending the white powdery crystals sailing up his nose.

For a few seconds, he just sat there, letting his head rest against the seat. Slowly, a smile began to develop and tug at the corners of his lips. " 'Operation Make Money.' I don't know why I hadn't thought of it before."

With that said, Eric revved the engine again, turned the heater on full blast, and burned rubber, leaving the warehouse in a cloud of dust in the distance.

# Chapter Nine

EMILY LAY DOWN ON HER bed, willing sleep to take her to a fantasy land of dreams. The butterflies kept dancing, fluttering through her stomach, though. Sleep eluded her. She was going to marry the man of her dreams tomorrow morning, so she really didn't have to dream of him anymore.

She wondered how she could have gotten so lucky. All she had ever wanted was someone like Eric to enter her life. Things were going to be like they should have always been for her.

Emily smiled wistfully as she thought how she had envied the girls in high school. All of their beautiful clothes and smiling faces. Of course, all of them liked her and almost put her on a pedestal. That was only because she never let anyone get close enough to really know her. No one ever knew what lay just below the surface.

Emily thought back to the time when she was a little girl and had read Cinderella for the first time. She had held the leather bound book tightly to her chest and said a quiet prayer that, one day, she too would meet her own Prince Charming, white horse and all. She had read the book over a hundred times and her Granny Millie told her all she ever had to do was believe in her dreams and they would come true. Of course, Emily knew she wasn't Cinderella. But, she had spent many nights wondering when her Prince Charming was going to come.

At last, she felt her eyelids grow heavy with sleep. Yes, Eric was her Prince. Wasn't he? She should have fallen into a deep relaxing sleep, secure in the knowledge that all of her worries were over. Eric would always care for her. She wouldn't have to fly anymore. She could be the wife and mother she had longed for most of her life. But the peaceful sleep she craved would not come. Questions. So many questions she had never asked.

As Emily began to think of the previous conversations, she tried hard to remember every detail, every little fact that Eric had thrown her way. There weren't many. He had no family. She had no family. She was lying. She wondered if he was lying, too.

Emily tried to wash away the fears that were beginning to fester within her. She didn't want to get cold feet. If Eric had a past like hers, then he needed her more than she could ever imagine. She knew he needed her. She could feel it in her bones. With that thought, Emily finally drifted off to sleep, although it was not a restful sleep.

THE SUN WAS SHINING BRIGHTLY when Emily awoke. She considered that a very good omen for Seattle. A sun filled beautiful wedding day. Who could ask for anything more?

"There is a God," Emily whispered before stretching her long limbs and swinging her legs from the bed. She began to hum, and then broke out into song: "I'm getting married in a few hours..."

She had so much to do. Emily ran a full tub of warm water. She added drops of rose oil and sprinkled three cupfuls of rose petals into the sweet smelling water. She sank beneath the warm ripples. Closing her eyes, she smiled wistfully, not believing her good fortune.

Eric. She loved him so much, and when nightfall came, she would be his wedded wife. She soaked in the water for more than an hour, keeping it toasty by continually running hot, steaming water into it. She kept the candles going and added two more cups of rose petals. She had told Eric not to call or come by. She planned on meeting him at the church promptly at three o'clock.

Emily had found the small church on the East side of town. Eric had wanted to get married at the courthouse but Emily had remained firm. She was only getting married once in her life. She could live without a bridesmaid, a long white gown, tuxes, a reception, and even a band. But, she could not live without a church, a bouquet, and some semblance of a honeymoon. Eric had finally agreed.

Emily had spent a month's salary on the winter white suit, which would serve as her wedding dress. It was a summer suit and the color had just the faintest hint of a pale yellow running through it. Chanel was Emily's favorite designer, and the moment she had laid eyes on it, she knew it was hers. She hadn't even bothered to look at the price tag. Her bouquet was a delicate arrangement of pink, yellow, and cream roses, mixed with an assortment of deep green ivy and baby's breath.

Emily had her hairdresser coming at eleven and her manicurist at noon. The professional makeup artist she had hired would be arriving shortly after one o'clock. The only real thing Emily had wanted and Eric absolutely would not allow was a photographer. She had even shed tears over the argument. But, he had convinced her that they didn't need to take pictures of an event that would forever be etched in their hearts and minds and souls. It had sounded so romantic when he had laid her down and made sweet love. Only now, it didn't make any sense to her and was the one thing she wished for. She wanted to record her joyous moment. To capture the looks on their faces as they exchanged their vows of love. But there would be no photographer. Emily was not about to upset her husband to be.

THE SMALL CHURCH WAS VERY still and quiet. The flowers Emily had selected created an understated elegance. The mixed bouquets of roses, peonies, and tulips adorned with delicate greenery filled cut glass vases that were placed at the altar and on the pulpit.

The old church held a quiet dignity. Its dark stained hardwood floors and massive beams spoke volumes about its past. Strong, sturdy, enduring. The delicately stained glassed windows adorned each side of the walls and served as drapes of beauty. For a moment, Emily just stared at the tiny church. It was beautiful. It was perfect. She patted down her elegant suit, flicking a speck of imaginary dust from her skirt. She inhaled, taking in the sweet scent of her own bouquet. The butterflies began to fly in her stomach. She was Cinderella, and this was her grand ballroom. Soon, her dashing prince would enter the side door and extend his hand to her and make her his wife. And they would live happily ever after.

Emily came out of her trance just as the diminutive pastor and his wife strode toward her. His face was kind and gentle and knowing. He took her hand and held it tightly for a moment. Emily stared into his deep pensive eyes, hoping to absorb some of their calmness.

"You look radiant, my dear," he said in a quiet, peaceful tone.

"More like an angel in white than a bride," echoed his wife. She was a heavyset woman nearing sixty, with bluish hair and an ill fitting suit. Her large plastic pearls accented her large neck, but her smile was as genuine as her well wishes.

"I'm sure you're just a bundle of nerves. Just a bundle of nerves. But don't you worry. It's all to be expected. Why, a beautiful young woman only walks down this aisle once in life. So don't you fret one bit. If you feel like crying, I've got a big shoulder. If you feel like laughing, I've got me a hearty laugh. But if you feel like running, then let's just run downstairs to the nursery and talk a minute," she said with a big grin.

Emily returned the woman's infectious smile. She truly liked these two people standing before her.  She was pleased she had found the church and Pastor Dan Ellis and his wife, Nelly. She had searched the telephone book for nondenominational churches and had discovered only a few existed in the area. Since Eric had insisted on rushing, she had been delighted when she'd opened the heavy double oak doors of "The Church of the Savior" and had known instantly that this was the place she wanted to be in her memory forever. This church, with all of its quiet reverend beauty, would be a part of Emily forever.

She had taken a moment to close her eyes and envisioned walking down the aisle. After meeting with the minister, she walked out of the church feeling at ease and proud of her discovery. Now, she stood once more at the threshold, waiting to walk down the aisle. But this time she wasn't imagining it, she was living it.

"Thank you both for all of your kind words, all of your help. The church looks lovely. I do so very much appreciate you," Emily said sincerely.

All three looked at the church's side door when it creaked open. Emily gasped. There stood Eric, regally dressed in a dove gray summer suit. Emily's eyes filled with tears of love.

"There, there," said Nelly. "Your husband to be doesn't want to see you cry!"

Emily smiled, "Of course he doesn't. I'm ready if you are."

On that cue, to Emily's surprise, Nelly walked away and sat at the organ. She proceeded to play the wedding march with all of her heart. Emily knew this was the best day of her life. She slowly stepped from the vestibule and began the short walk to Eric's waiting extended hand. She held his hand lightly, looking into his eyes. She loved him deeply, and she was ready for a new life.

# Chapter Ten

EMILY HAD DREAMED AND CHOREOGRAPHED her wedding day for as long as she could remember. The ceremony itself would be handwritten. Vows would be uttered with an intense sincerity and the mood would be solemn yet genuine. Emily had long ago determined that she would savor every moment of the occasion, listening intently as her beloved spoke eloquently of his shared love and admiration for her. Emily startled herself as she dove out of her dreamy world and back into reality, while her real beloved, Eric, stood before her, quickly and impatiently whizzing through his I do's.

The ceremony was brief and shortened by Eric's rapid fire responses. As soon as "I do" was exchanged, Eric pecked her on the lips with a perfunctory kiss, and turned on his heels to leave. Emily hugged Pastor Dan warmly and smiled sweetly to his wife. She realized right then that she was embarrassed by her own wedding ceremony. She pressed a crisp fifty dollar bill into Nelly's hand. "This is for the offering plate on Sunday," she whispered apologetically.

As man and wife, Emily and Eric departed the church and entered the limousine that Eric had waiting. Sensing Emily's unease, Eric popped a bottle of fine champagne and gazed deeply into her eyes. "To my bride. My wife. Mrs. Eric Blake," he cooed as he raised his crystal fluted glass upwards in a toast to her.

With those words spoken, Emily easily forgot her own displeasure and was filled with a giddy little girl happiness. She wondered deeply, wanting to know what it was within herself that made her always try to find something wrong in everything. She shook away the anxious feeling and let the tide of pleasure rush over her.

My wife, Mrs. Eric Blake. She loved the sound of those words.

She sipped the chilled fine wine and leaned against the soft leather seat. "That happens to be the loveliest thing anyone has ever called me," she sighed. Eric took her in his arms and kissed her passionately. "Then let's let the honeymoon begin."

The honeymoon, Emily thought. She had wanted to take an exotic trip for the honeymoon, but Eric had explained an extended expensive trip would have to wait. Emily thought back to just days before when Eric had taken a deep breath and asked Emily to please sit down.

"It is difficult for me, Emily, to bare this all to you since you hold me in such high regard." Emily had urged him to please bare his soul and all of his worries to her. She held his head and gently slid her fingers through his beautiful black hair as he slowly let the story unfold.

Painstakingly, he apologized for letting Emily down. For soon, as man and wife, a true couple, they would begin their life with a problem. He had maintained it was his problem and one he alone would solve. Eric explained how his business had been faltering, and he even alluded that he was worried about his job security. He had tenderly told Emily he didn't want to burden her because he knew he would work it all out. He assured her that life would be back on track and normal very soon.

"So, it breaks my heart to have to share such information, because it makes me feel a failure even before our marriage and our sweet life together can begin," he confided to her.

"I know asking you to marry me in such a rush, when my business is off and I can't offer you the world, is selfish of me. I love you Emily. I just want that one good thing going in my life. You. You will make my life rich and full."

But Emily hadn't been so sure. She certainly didn't want Eric to suffer or worry about her.

"Eric, I have money saved. I have a very healthy portfolio. We could borrow against it or something. I mean, just until you're back on your feet. That's why I have the money," she pleaded.

"I've always said it was for a rainy day. So sweetheart, if it's going to rain on our parade for a little while, let's stop the rain and bring out the sunshine. You can repay me or the loan when all of your business straightens back up. Of course, whatever is mine is yours. You never have to repay me," she laughed. "It would be like repaying yourself!"

Eric had steadfastly and stubbornly refused her offer. But Emily had not let up. She practically begged him. It took less than forty eight hours for Eric to agree. They entered her broker's office, signed all of the papers as husband and wife to be, and his name was added to all of her accounts. Emily was elated at being able to help. She had felt pride. Eric had felt relief.

When the disappointment of not being able to take a real honeymoon had worn off, Emily finally succumbed and accepted the idea of postponing it for the time being. As a compromise, she settled on a romantic weekend at the very exclusive "Baron Estates." Emily laughed as Eric swung her into his arms, carrying her over the threshold of their suite.

"Oh Eric, it's lovely. And more champagne?" Emily read the card from the hotel's manager, "Best wishes Mr. and Mrs. Eric Blake. Isn't that nice?"

Filled with wine and the sheer joy of happiness, Emily collapsed in Eric's waiting arms. "Kiss me and love me, always," she whispered. Eric held her tightly; not wanting to let her go as he slowly began to make love to his wife.

Arching her back, stretching, Emily gazed at her husband. His sleepy eyes returned her stare through half slits. She ran her long fingers over his bare chest. "There's still so much to do. I mean, planning a wedding practically overnight and then actually getting married, and all of a sudden here we are. But where do we go from here?" Emily asked.

"Whatever do you mean, my sweet?" Eric said as he nibbled her ear.

"I mean, I can't go on living in my apartment, and you can't live there, and we certainly can't live forever in your hotel room. Are we moving to Pennsylvania and do I have to quit work and…?"

Eric put his finger to her lips. "Emily, first of all, you need to keep working at least for a while. I told you that my job is not secure right now. Secondly, I must work harder and be gone more to change my current situation. Third, we will not be moving to Pennsylvania, and I have no idea why you would ever think that 'we' would. Just because I am based there does not mean that I need my wife there, too."

The words stung Emily. She felt her throat constrict. "Where do you plan on us living?" Eric moved her head from its resting place. "No changes as of right now."

He started to continue but could feel her stiffen at his touch. "Perhaps in the next few weeks you could start looking for a small apartment for us."

Emily eased. Her growing tension began to leave her body. Of course, he couldn't just buy a house. His business was in trouble. She was already nagging. She just hoped he would forgive her.

"I'm sorry darling. Whatever it takes, I can handle it. I will look for something small and inexpensive, but there's no hurry." Emily arched her long neck and kissed his soft lips. She was content once again in his arms. Eric smiled over her head, thinking what his next step would be.


ERIC CRUISED DOWN THE DESERTED alleyway, slowly checking each number on the filth-laden doors, searching for the right one. Creeping to a stop, he checked his watch and then eased down low in the seat.

Carefully, he pulled the gleaming Colt .45 from his waistband. He touched the weapon as if it were made of gold. That's how Eric felt about his prized possession of the moment. Without this companion, he wouldn't be here. He checked the chamber, spun it, and snapped it back in place. With expert care, he laid it in his lap.

Pulling a pack of cigarettes from his coat pocket, Eric scanned the alleyway again for any signs of life. He lit the cigarette and let the smoke curl from his lips. He took long deep drags as the embers lit the inside of the darkened car. Except for the occasional drags on the burning stick in his mouth, Eric didn't move. He was an animal ready to strike. Coiled tightly, watching his prey.

A young man stepped out of the back alley door. A tie-dyed shirt, jeans, and sandals were his uniform. A small brown paper sack was tucked under his arm, rolled and taped tightly with masking tape.

The young man, Jean Louis, nervously glanced from side to side. The alley was narrow. He looked directly at Eric's car and nodded. Eric didn't move. He sat there watching Jean Louis as he started toward him, and Jean Louis only hesitated for a brief second before opening the passenger's side door and sliding in.

Seeing the gun, Jean Louis let out a low whistle. "I guess you don't believe in peace, huh, man."

Eric brushed him off. "Yeah, I believe in piece. That's why I brought mine with me.

Jean Louis loosened up a little with the light joke. "That's funny man."

"Yeah, well, great. I'm glad you're amused. Do you have something for me or not?"

Jean Louis placed the brown wrapped package on the seat. Eric picked it up and shook his head. "I wish you wouldn't tape it like this. It's too hard to check it out in the car."

The young man just shrugged, not really caring if Eric was inconvenienced. "Your package is under the seat. Get it and get out. If anything is wrong with my shipment, you're ass is grass. And not the kind of crap you smoke all the time. Got it?" Eric barked.

"Yeah, man. I got it." Jean Louis reached for the door handle and opened the car door, flipping his long hair over his shoulders, still clutching the envelope from Eric. He turned to him, and said, "You know man, you need to learn to be cool. Get with the groove. You're too..."

With those words spoken, Eric pumped two bullets into Jean Louis's head, causing him to reel backwards out of the car as the envelope landed on the seat. Eric smiled and leaned over to shut the door. He took the envelope and put it back into his coat pocket, lit another cigarette, and started the car. The noise of the engine filled the quiet of the night. He looked in his rearview mirror, adjusted it, and sped away; leaving Jean Louis's body sprawled across the door step.

# Chapter Eleven

EMILY HAD ALWAYS BEEN THANKFUL FOR her job at the airline. She loved the heady experiences she lived every day. And, although flying had become a deeply rooted part of who she was and had boosted her self esteem, she knew that being a wife was the role in life she had always wanted. Plain and simple. Emily was flying high on life and loving it because she was genuinely happy. Eric made her happy.

As soon as Emily's flight schedule was posted, she would give it to Eric and somehow he would always manage to have those very days free. He was the perfect husband, bearing small gifts and fresh flowers each time he saw her after her trips. Emily grew to love him more with each passing day. She had never realized she had the capacity to love someone so deeply.

It had taken her three months to gather enough courage to bring up the apartment idea again. She had planned her words carefully and, in true Emily fashion, had thoroughly done her homework, having secretly looked at dozens of apartments. If she was going to work, they could afford a nice two bedroom with a lovely view of the river. Emily had seen enough cheap apartments to know she didn't plan on living in one. She would use some of her savings if she had to.

The apartment Emily found would be perfect for their needs. She still had easy access to the airport and bus lines, if it ever came to that. Otherwise, she could still take a taxi to and from work. She could furnish the apartment by going to secondhand shops. There were dozens of them in the downtown area. She could also go to garage sales. Emily was excited about her project. Now she just hoped Eric would join her in her excitement.

Emily sighed, looking at her watch. She had a lot to do to get ready to see Eric. She would not allow herself to rush. She never wanted Eric to see her except at her very best. If it took her an extra hour, then he would have to wait. Emily would always be meticulous when it came to her looks, and even more so now that she was married.

"I will never disappoint you, Eric. Because I know you will never disappoint me." Emily smiled, thinking about the new apartment. Yes, another adventure and another new road to go down together.

If she had her own apartment, she wouldn't have to take the time to get a taxi downtown. Emily felt frustrated and she didn't feel it was quite right that she had to go to a hotel when Eric came to town.

"After all," she told herself, "I am married to the man. I am not the mistress." The truth was, she was sick and tired of continuing to live with other women, although they seldom saw one another. She was sick and tired of living a life as a part-time wife. She wanted a home. She wanted all the trimmings. She wanted Eric to have a place to come home to. She wanted to cook him meals. She wanted to have a life.

Emily began to feel her resolve weaken at the thought of telling him. What if he didn't agree? What if he wanted to keep things the way they were, with him living in one city and her in another, and then the two of them in hotels? Emily could not do it any longer. Eric would have to agree.

Emily would never cross Eric, but this was very important to her. She decided to get the apartment, decorate it, and then surprise him with it for their fourth month anniversary. Knowing this was truly the best decision for her and for Eric in the long run, she felt her spirits rise. She could see it all now: a beautiful little apartment with linen curtains and a rose petal design on the bedspread covering a big queen sized bed of cherry. She would really have to scout the discount markets. Emily had a new mission and was truly happy once again.


"THANK YOU SO MUCH. It's perfect." Emily was beside herself with pleasure. She had found the perfect apartment in less than a week. She had started with the Queene Anne district and then headed to Beacon

Hill. Each area afforded great views of the water and mountains. She loved the area around Magnolia and Queene Anne. The houses were a mixture of elegance on one corner and plainness on the next. She liked the mixture. When she walked into the stunning little apartment complex she could feel her excitement level rise. When she actually entered the apartment that was advertised for rent, she knew she was home.

The apartment manager, Karen, looked at Emily and smiled. "Well, I hope you all will be happy. You know, if you need anything, I'm home most of the time. Apartment 3-A. Just ring the bell." Karen was an attractive woman in her mid-thirties, and Emily already felt a close bond with her.

"I will, and thanks again. I appreciate you letting me have it so quickly. It's going to knock your socks off when I finish it."

Emily rushed back to her apartment complex and barely made it before Eric pulled up in front to say his good-byes. "I'll miss you, Mrs. Blake. Stay sweet." Eric nuzzled her neck and tenderly kissed her soft lips.

"Soon, my sweet." Emily waved as she watched the taillights of the car fade in the distance. Secretly, she was excited to see him go.

"No time this week to enjoy a pity party. I have another kind of party to go to, and it's called decorating."

She headed straight to the apartment complex. She could move in two weeks. Emily wasted no time. She only had three more days off and would have to take some vacation time without Eric knowing. That shouldn't be hard. Eric seldom called when she was on call, and she really never knew where he was. She only knew that he was working very hard to land some big clients and his traveling was extensive.

ERIC WAS TIRED. HE WHIPPED HIS Ford Torino into the deserted warehouse parking area, sending dust and gravel flying. It was hard to imagine that so much had happened since he had last been summoned to the warehouse.

Eric patted his pocket filled with cash. Now he had both their money and their dope.  At least he had what he thought was theirs. According to his calculations, he had just the right amount. Eric could just hear the old man now: "Ah, but Eric, there is such a thing as interest. And I have been so patient." Screw the old man.

He revved the engine once, and then all went quiet. Too quiet. Rolling down his window, Eric glanced nervously around him. There was no sign of life. No birds were singing. No planes were flying overhead. No trucks on nearby lots. No other cars entering into the warehouse for the meeting. No nothing.  Just silence. Just plain silence filled the air, filled his head, and filled everything.

Absentmindedly, Eric wiped the small beads of sweat forming on his brow. He adjusted the rearview mirror and studied his reflection carefully. Staring back at him was a desperate man. Staring back at him was a dead man.

Eric began to shake violently. As he shook, the realization of what was about to happen hit him hard, like a brick being thrown full force into his chest. Eric knew he only had seconds to live. And he decided to do just that. He wasn't going to be set up, take the fall, and be the patsy for these suckers.

He knew they were somewhere in the darkness, watching him, waiting for him to get out of the car so they could pump his body with their bullets. Eric tried to breathe. He had to get focused. He had to think. It seemed as if hours had dragged by when in reality only a few seconds had passed.

With shaking hands, Eric reached into his pocket and as casually as possible, took out his cigarettes. Lighting one, he inhaled deeply, letting the smoke curl from his lips before he made small round circles. As one hand held his cigarette, the other slowly and carefully reached for the ignition key. In a fluid motion of guts and glory, Eric turned the ignition and slammed his foot on the accelerator, catapulting the car forward, with tires spinning and gravel being thrown high into the air.

Eric drove like a demon possessed. They would not kill him. He was there to make good on his debt. He was there to settle the score. Now they had decided they wanted his blood. Eric slammed his fist against the steering wheel. He drove fast and furious out of the industrial park, leaving only dust, gravel, and what he knew were disappointed, angry faces of evil men behind. He would show them. Nobody was going to screw Eric Blake. Yes, he would be the one that got away. He would be the one that got away and lived to tell about it.

Ten miles down the road, he finally spotted a gas station. His hands were now steady, and plans were spinning in his head. All he needed was to get away for a while. He needed to lay low and get his thoughts together. He needed to figure out his next course of action. He needed to get high. First, he would call Emily. Then he'd get high. That always made him think better. No, he'd get high first.

Eric took the small plastic bag from the glove compartment box and untwisted the wire. Using his pocket knife, he carefully dipped it into the white powder, extracting a small mound, which he held close to his nostril. Inhaling deeply, Eric let the white powder work it's magic on him. He calmly lit another cigarette and looked at himself in the rearview mirror again. This time he smiled back at his reflection. He wasn't a dead man. He was alive and well and loving it. And he planned on remaining that way.


EMILY PACED AROUND THE LIVING room. She smoothed her well coifed hair and looked at her beautifully manicured hands. She wanted Eric to call so she could tell him where to meet her. She had decided tonight was the night. Not one more night in a hotel room as a married couple. It was ridiculous.

The small but beautifully furnished apartment would change his mind. She had excelled at everything. She had found the perfect couch, but had paid so little for it that no one would ever know she hadn't spent a small fortune. She had written checks for more than she had planned. But, who wanted to sleep on cheap sheets? And who would use anything but high quality towels? Not me, thought Emily.

She had been fortunate enough to find an older couple moving out of her apartment complex and into a retirement home. They had lovely pieces of antiques that would have made any home beautiful. Emily had bought their hand carved, solid cherry, four poster bed. The armoire itself made a statement of wealth, luxury, and abundance. She had also bought a cherry dining room set from them that would make most women turn green with envy.

The table had intricate inlaid pieces of darker cherry wood crisscrossing in lighter shades, creating a subtle sunburst design from the center. Emily knew the table should have cost one hundred times more than what she had actually paid for it. She knew it. The retiring couple did not. But they had been happy with the large check Emily had given them. One lump sum from such a nice young married girl starting out on her own with her new husband had actually made the older couple happy.

Emily had made the move over the weekend. She had been off reserve for some time, so she now knew her schedule in advance, which was like a dream come true. She could now make plans and not have to change them because of her work schedule. When the telephone finally did ring, Emily jumped. How long had she been pacing and thinking of her little slice of heaven just a few miles away?

She answered the telephone coolly: "Hello."

Eric purred into the receiver. "Hello, my pet. And how are you this fine evening?"

"I'm fine, now that you've called. Listen instead of meeting you at the hotel, I have a surprise. Take down this address and I'll meet you there in one hour."

Eric wasn't looking to play games. He'd had enough games for one day. "What's this about, Emily? I'm tired. I've been on the road. I am ready to see you now. Do you understand?" he said, a little too harshly.

Emily was not to be deterred. "Yes, I understand Eric. But, just trust me on this one. The address is 206 Tennessee Avenue. Number 1-A. Got it?"

Eric didn't like it, but he agreed, "Yeah, I got it. I don't know what you're up to, but it better be good."

Emily sat down on the couch she had shared with the other women. Thinking back on the last two years, she realized she didn't know them any better than she did those she worked with. They weren't the caliber of people she wanted to be around. Not yet anyway.

One other stewardess had married an extremely wealthy man. He owned real estate property all over the world, and she had quickly quit her job to begin traveling with him. Emily had heard she was already pregnant with their first child. Another colleague had married a professional football player. They now lived in New York and were enjoying the good life. Emily was planning on looking both of these women up and pursuing their friendship. Their husbands might be helpful to Eric, plus she wanted to be around other married women who had been like herself, able to fall in love and marry a wealthy man.

Being a stewardess was the most glamorous job she could think of. She was respected, yet men flirted shamelessly with her. She smiled her way into many hearts. But she had already succeeded in love. She was a married woman. She was just glad the company allowed stewardesses to get married. Just a few short years ago that would have been unheard of.

Of course, getting pregnant was another thing. The company would never allow that. If one wanted a quick and sure way to lose their job, then one would just get pregnant. With that thought, Emily smiled. Yes, she knew what she was doing. She knew it was for the best. If not for Eric, it was certainly the best for her.


WHEN ERIC ARRIVED AT THE APARTMENT complex he studied it closely. If Emily had arranged dinner with another couple, he thought he would kill her. But he couldn't think who they knew that would ask them to dinner.

Since their marriage, Eric's life had been spiraling out of control. He was sure that Emily noticed. Just an hour earlier he had hoped to solve some of his problems. But no. The powers that be had decided a different fate for Eric.

He circled the building. He needed to hide, not socialize. He parked his burgundy four-door Torino in the back of the building and walked around to the front. At least no one would know where to look for him while he was here.

Eric slowly approached the apartment looking over his shoulder, checking to make sure no one, absolutely no one, was behind him. The fleeting thought of how long he would have to keep checking over his shoulder entered his mind. Forever, he concluded.

He knocked softly on the door. Emily immediately swung the door open, wearing the sheerest most seductive pink negligee he had ever seen. It barely covered her perfect body. Her blonde hair was swept up high and her face was radiant. He stood speechless. "Welcome home, darling," Emily cooed.

With those words, Eric cocked his head to one side, "Home?"

"Yes, dear I said 'home.' Come inside. I've got lots to show and tell you."

Eric stepped over the threshold and surveyed the room. It was, as with everything Emily did, impeccable. Only the best.

"Excuse me, dear, but did you say 'home?' " Eric asked again.

"Yes, Eric. I know you said not to do anything just yet. But you did tell me to start looking. This just fell into my lap and it was the best price, and I got all of this stuff at great prices, too. I know you must be tired of living in hotels and..."

Eric shut her up with kisses. He smiled, because she had given him the perfect hideaway. The old man and his cronies didn't know about Emily, and they certainly wouldn't know about this place. He didn't even know about it until two minutes ago.

Things were going to be changing, but for right now, this was perfect. In fact, things couldn't be better. But Eric knew he had to move quickly. Emily was stunned, but happy.

"You mean you like it? I mean, it's OK? I mean, oh I don't know what I mean, except that I love you to the moon and back!"

They fell into each other's arms. They were each in their own world, clinging and pulling each other into unknown territory. They clung to each other, hoping to somehow find what they were looking for. But, neither of them had any idea where they were headed.

# Chapter Twelve

HAVING FLOWN AND HAVING STAYED IN hotel rooms for her layovers for the past seven straight days, Emily was exhausted. But her spirits began to lift as she turned the key into the lock. She wanted nothing more than to be at home with Eric. To wrap her tired arms around him and smell his sweet scent. She wanted to be no other place in the world but home. Home. That one simple word sounded so sweet to Emily's tired mind.

She had called for the last three days whenever she could and had never been able to reach Eric. She said a silent prayer, hoping he hadn't been called out of town on business and was unable to reach her. She flipped the light switch and froze. Her heart began to pound. Someone had broken in. Someone had ransacked her belongings. The small but usually well-kept apartment looked as if a twister had roared through at high speed. As Emily gingerly stepped over clothing and empty plates, it dawned on her. Nothing was missing.

Eric staggered from the bedroom and Emily heard herself gasp. He was unshaven and smelled. Giving her a lopsided grin, he managed to speak. "Hello my dear, welcome home." He gestured wildly, throwing his arms out wide and bowing.

Emily's eyes burned with fury. "What do you mean by this?" she demanded.

Eric stared at her for half of a second before responding. With a smirk, he simply said, "Emily shut up. Don't yell at me now, or ever. You got that?"

Emily felt her fury escape her reason as she fled toward him, ready to strike. But he struck first, slamming her against the wall. Her hand went to her mouth, and she tasted blood.

"Why you bastard! How dare you hit me," Emily seethed. "I've been gone a week. You haven't touched a thing. This place is filthy. You're filthy. And then you hit me?" she yelled.

Eric looked at her unconcerned. "Yeah, that's right. You think you're so smart, making all the damn decisions. Then welcome to the real world, baby. You wanted me home with you, now you got me home with you."

Eric turned and went back into the bedroom, slamming, then locking, the door behind him. Emily slowly rose from her crumbled position. She was dazed and confused. Was this a dream or was this a nightmare that was truly happening? She wiped at her mouth again, taking care the blood did not get on her clothes or the carpet.

She staggered into the kitchen. Dishes, wine bottles, and glasses with lipstick around them filled the sink. There were no clean dishes. Emily looked around in bewilderment. How could this be happening?

In the bedroom, Eric laid another line of the fine white powder on the mirror. He took a twenty dollar bill and rolled it tightly. He held the makeshift straw to the powder and inhaled, snorting all of it into his nostril in one quick movement. He did the same with the second line of fine powder.

Emily marched to the bedroom door and tried the doorknob. It was locked. She slammed her fist against the door. "Eric, open the door now, you son of a bitch. This apartment is in my name and you can't do this."

Eric swung the door open wide. "This apartment is in Mrs. Eric Blake's name. You are MY wife and I can do anything the hell I want. Now, I don't like sleeping with anyone when I am like this. You sleep on the beautiful sofa you wanted so badly. I'll take the bed. And Emily, don't bother me." With that said, he slammed the door in her face.


EMILY SLEPT ON THE COUCH FOR THE next three nights. Eric would retreat from the room, leave for an hour and return, only to return back to the room and lock the door. What had happened to turn this person around so quickly? Emily, for one, had no idea.

She knew the entire situation had made her sick to her stomach. She had thrown up every day since she had been home. The queasy feeling wouldn't go away. "He's actually made me sick," she thought.

She was sick enough to call the airline and tell them she couldn't work, but deep down she knew it would be better to get away. Perhaps, whatever was happening to Eric, whatever was going on in his life, would be straightened out, and hopefully he would get it back together when she returned. She hoped for her sake that he would. She knew she couldn't live like this. Emily gathered her clothes and uniforms and left Eric a note.

"*My darling Eric,*

*I don't understand what has come over you. I love you and want to help. I know you aren't yourself and there must be a great amount of pressure on you from your job for you to act like this. But please, remember that I am your wife. I am your partner and will always stand by you. I forgive you for striking me, but Eric, don't ever touch me again like that. I love you, but we need to talk. I will return in six days. Love, Emily.*"

Placing the note on the bedroom door with tape, Emily gently laid her hand on the fine paper. She sighed, wondering how her life had spiraled so completely and honestly out of control. And she wondered why. Why when happiness had been captured and she was experiencing a dream she had dreamed of all of her life. She had fallen deeply in love and had married the man of her dreams. Why should she once again have to delve into a nightmare?

She wanted to awaken from this. "Please God. Let it be okay." Emily took a deep breath and steadied herself as she walked out of the apartment, only guessing what fate would deal her next.

⤳ ✺ ⤳

ERIC FOUND THE NOTE QUITE AMUSING AND laughed heartily out loud. How childish. How stupid. A note. Just like Emily to leave a note. She just didn't get it. Eric chuckled. "She'll be getting it soon enough, that's for sure."

He was the king of the castle and this was his castle, after all. He could do whatever he wanted. And he had decided he didn't like the furniture she had bought. "Yes. A sale is in order. Everything must go," he bellowed, to no one but beautifully painted and covered walls. Eric quickly assessed the situation and decided he was in need of some more cocaine, since his stash was getting dangerously low. And he knew that would never do. No, never.

HE HADN'T SLEPT. HIS EYES were roadmaps of drugs. His hair stuck to his head from the dirt and grease. He hadn't changed clothes in a week. But he felt quite comfortable in his new role of drug addict and man of the house. It all seemed perfectly normal to him.

Why should he care if his business was all but gone? He had Emily. Dear sweet Emily had pulled him out of all of his messes. Eric thought of the old man trying to find him. He had been spotted a few times around town when he had ventured out to buy more drugs. But no one knew where Eric vanished each time as he slipped from their sights. Yes. Emily was his savior.

"Yes, when she comes back home I'll kiss her and tell her how much I love her for helping me. If only I could stand up," he groaned from the bed.

He needed one more line, he thought. Grabbing the pouch, he scattered the dust on the table, snorting it quickly with a straw. As the white powder traveled through his blood and the feeling of euphoria once again took over his being, Emily walked through the door. He lifted the heavy lids of his eyes and tried to focus. He knew she was standing there. He could almost make out her pretty violet dress. Her hair was pulled back tightly against her neck. His Emily looked pretty, but she looked sick. She was pale. God, Eric thought, don't tell me she's going to cry again.

Emily studied Eric only briefly. Her mind raced forward and then backwards. What was happening in her life?

"I might as well go ahead and die," Emily whispered, as a tear slid down her cheek.

Just then, Eric reached out for her. His thin, bare arms begged to her. She stood motionless, taking in the sight. He whimpered, his voice ravaged with drugs, raspy.

"Emily, my darling, I'm sorry. I need your help. Please forgive me." With that, she rushed to his arms and began sobbing. But she was not crying for herself, or for Eric, but for the unborn child that was growing inside of her.

They lay in each other's arms for more than an hour. Finally, Emily sought the courage to speak. "Eric I don't understand it. I know you're on drugs. The signs of them are everywhere. The plastic bags, the powder."

She stopped in mid-sentence. She looked around the room she had only half seen when she had walked through the door just one hour ago and fallen into his pleading, pitiful arms. Her beautiful dining room table and chairs and buffet and china cabinets were all gone. She slowly rose and walked into the bedroom, which was empty, except for a mattress on the floor. She walked back into the living room and looked at the spot where her beautiful couch had once been. In its place was a shabby secondhand piece from a dumpster.

From that point on, Emily knew nothing but hatred. She whirled around, ready to spit at Eric, but he was standing facing her, full of strength. "What, you don't like something?" Emily didn't know what to say. Her world had just completely fallen all around her, and only she was left standing with nothing else.

Instinctively, she held her hand to her stomach. "Oh Eric, how could you? I'm pregnant. Pregnant with our child, and you've done all of this."

Eric exploded. He grabbed her by both arms and shook her violently, screaming. "Pregnant? Are you so stupid that you could get pregnant? You bitch! You whore! You idiot!"

He ranted and raved and then he turned toward her with a look in his eyes she had never witnessed before. He walked up to her and struck her hard in the stomach. Emily doubled over in pain and, just as she was about to catch her breath, he dealt her another full blow. Falling back, she hit her head against the table and her world faded to black.

# Chapter Thirteen

*A* HALLOW VACUUM WHIRLED DEEP WITHIN Emily. She could hear something, but she didn't know the sound. Was it silence fringed with echoes? No. It was beeps and tones and echoes. And darkness. Everything was black. As she tried to open her eyes, she realized it was taking more energy than she could gather. When she finally let them slide open slightly, the harsh light that greeted her hurt. Slowly, letting her eyes adjust, she shook her head. Nothing made sense to her right now. Where was she? Where was Eric?

Then, the realization of what had happened came gushing forward, exploding into her consciousness. Quickly clearing the cobwebs of drugs from her mind, her hand flew to her stomach. The pain was instant. Her body ached and the pain seared through to her soul.

"I have to get up, I have to get up." Emily knew she was speaking but couldn't even hear her own words. She tried to raise her thin, weak frame from the bed, but the pain overcame her. Gasping for breath, she again tried to speak. Her voice was low, course, and ravaged. Her words, unintelligible.

She looked around and the memories of what had happened flooded her very being. Tears welled in her eyes and threatened to spill onto her face. She would be brave. She looked around and knew where she was. She was in a stark white hospital room. And she was alone. Her lower lip trembled and her hands shook. She wanted to scream and she wanted to run blindly through the halls and shout the terror and horror of what had happened to her. But she lay there, motionless.

Emily turned as a portly grime-faced woman in a crisp white nurse's uniform entered the room. The woman casually eyed Emily and compassion was totally absent. In fact, for a brief moment, Emily thought she saw disdain in the woman's vacant stare. She was certain she didn't see kindness or understanding oozing from her.

The nurse edged closer to Emily and glared at her from her bedside. Roughly, she began to fluff her pillow and straighten her sheets. Emily could feel the rough hands poke and move her as her body screamed out for them to stop. But Emily said not a word. She just listened in amazement.

"Oh, I see we have decided to wake up. Your husband brought you in two days ago. Your fall down the stairs, in your excitement after purchasing cocaine, has caused you to miscarry, Little Miss. Your husband was beside himself. Why, he looked dead tired, as if he had to be up with you for days on end over your little adventures. I could tell he hadn't slept in days because of you. Why for the life of me a man like that would scurry around after you. Cleaning up after you, and here you are. Well, I just don't know what the world is coming to," she scolded.

Emily tried to speak, but the nurse cut her off, dismissing her as an evil child who had forsaken her parents.

"He left yesterday on very important business and said he would return tomorrow. I am glad you are going to be all right, Madame. But, personally, if I had a husband as kind and gentle and caring as yours, and had done what you did, I would leave you in a heartbeat. Now, the doctor will be in in about twenty minutes."

With that, the woman turned her back on Emily, scribbled something on the chart, which hung from Emily's bed, and marched from the room.

Emily felt the sting of tears hit her face. How could he dare do this? She would get her revenge. She would not let this go unsettled.

It was of little surprise to Emily that Eric never returned to the hospital. She was sure the only reason he had come in the first place was to plant his seeds of deceit. Had he even thought she might awaken and defend herself he would have left immediately and not stuck around for a full day. She was sure he had hoped to stick around long enough to watch her die. But at least she had disappointed him.

Emily gathered her few belongings and stuffed them into the brown paper bag. This was not what she had dreamed of when she had first learned of her pregnancy.

As the warm sunshine touched her face, Emily looked back at the hospital doors closing behind her. Another ending to another chapter, she thought bitterly.

A cab sidled up to the curb and sat idling. Emily opened the door and sluggishly climbed inside. The thick aroma of cigar smoke hit her in the face. Her stomach rolled into her throat and she was barely able to whisper her address to the man. She leaned against the green vinyl seat and let her breath escape her. An audible sigh slipped from her lips.

Each step out of the hospital's doors had been a task. Each step had been filled with a searing pain. She recounted the walk, her head held high as the nurses and doctors watched her walk out. They thought her something she wasn't. It had been that way her whole life, she thought grimly.

Emily paid the fare and struggled to her front door, just as a light rain began to fall. She fumbled with her keys and finally got the key to go into the lock, but it wouldn't turn. It was stuck. Placing her bags at the top of the steps, Emily had to find every ounce of energy just to make it down to the first floor again to find the manager's office.

Karen sat behind a small blond oak desk. Noticing Emily slumped in the doorway, she genuinely looked surprised to her.

"Well I knew you wouldn't run out on me like that."

Looking confused, Emily smiled. "I wasn't running anywhere. I've been in the hospital."

Karen raised her eyebrows and chose her words carefully. "Emily, you've only lived here a few months and already you're behind a month's rent. You move out in the middle of the night, you forfeit the deposit, you don't tell me anything, and now you tell me you've been in the hospital like nothing has happened? Come on, give me a break! I mean I have all of your clothes to hold as collateral, and some very nice ones at that, but Emily, you owe me a lot of money right now. You signed a one year lease and you know the penalties for breaking the lease."

Karen droned on, but Emily had quit listening to her a long time ago. She thought she was going to faint, but instead, she felt her strength returning.

"Karen, this may be hard to believe. I have no idea what you're talking about. If you have my clothes, you damn well better give them to me right now or I will have a lawyer on your back so quick your head won't quit spinning for weeks. For whatever I owe you, you will be paid. I don't know when. I have plenty of money in the bank and in stocks. You'll get your money. Right now, give me my clothes. I have a divorce to take care of."

Karen took a step back toward the wall, almost afraid of this young woman who had entered her office defeated and was now ready to do battle against the world. She wasn't sure if she was afraid or very impressed by her. She thought it was probably the latter.

"Sure, Emily," Karen said. "They're right back here. I mean, the apartment was completely empty, except for your clothes. I'm sorry. I didn't know what was going on."

Emily retorted back, "Yeah, well neither did I."

# Chapter Fourteen

THE BUTTERFLIES IN EMILY'S STOMACH would not be still. She took another deep breath. Strangely enough, she was almost excited about what lay ahead of her. Her high heels clicked hard on the concrete sidewalk as she made her way down the streets of Seattle. She stopped in front of a sixteen story building that was perfectly situated among the retail stores and the business district. It was a very formidable address. Most of the high rises that dotted the Seattle skyline were newly built. Since 1965, when The Boeing Company had come to the city, the economy had exploded with more than 100,000 workers moving in. New people with new homes and new labor and new business and skyscrapers had been popping up ever since. Emily patted down her suit and stepped inside.

It was precisely ten in the morning when Emily breezed into the law offices of Shane and Worthington. Of course, Emily had researched dozens of lawyers. She had done her homework as always. Emily had spent hours the day before researching various attorneys and making dozens of telephone calls to the local judicial bar, as well as the national bar association. She knew she not only wanted the best attorney available, but she had to have the best.

She wanted Eric's blood. She wanted alimony. She wanted to sue him for cruel and inhuman treatment. She wanted his company notified as to what he had done to her. She wanted him to pay her and she wanted to ruin him in the process.

The foyer of the law office spoke volumes about the gentlemen whose names it bore. Rich mahogany furniture filled the outer office, along with tapestry hangings and original artwork. Wingback chairs, embossed in a thick floral pattern, faced each other, and small hand embroidered footstools with intricate cravings adorning their tiny feet were placed nearby. A sterling silver tea service was quietly, yet proudly, displayed on a side buffet, and only the latest reading material lay on the Chinese beveled glass coffee table.

An attractive woman in a nubile soft yellow suit greeted Emily. "Hello, Mrs. Blake. May I get you anything? Coffee? Tea? Perhaps a soft drink?"

Emily shook her head and smiled. "I'll just wait, thank you."

The young woman retreated behind the double mahogany doors. The soft music, which made for easy listening, filled the foyer. Emily relaxed. She was doing the right thing. The quicker she could get this over with, the better. She would go back to work and start life again. She was sure she had enough in savings to cover herself for a good while. At least she hadn't quit her job.

The small, pleasant young woman re-entered the room, "Mr. Shane will see you now, Mrs. Blake. Please follow me." Emily followed her through the doors into the rich inner sanctum of the back offices. More than a dozen beautifully dressed secretaries were busy typing. She liked the feel of the office. It was classy and elegant.

She was confident with her choice. Emily herself had carefully prepared herself for the meeting. As always, she had her hair fixed before the meeting, making sure it was at its absolute best. Her nails were perfect, and she had chosen a pale blue Chanel suit with matching pumps and bag. The pale blue set off her lovely hair and blue eyes. She could have walked right off the cover of Vogue magazine and she knew it. Who would have ever guessed that two days earlier she was lying in a hospital bed, struggling to overcome severe obstacles after being beaten one week ago today, which resulted in the loss of her baby?

The door opened into a larger office. Emily had to catch her breath. The office was enormous. The windows stretched from floor to ceiling, exposing the beautiful Seattle landscape far below. Emily could see small tugboats vying for attention as they plowed up and down The Puget Sound. She took in the calming view, and then surveyed her surroundings.

There were two sitting areas. One was more intimate than the other. No, Emily decided, it was more feminine. It consisted of two small wingback antique chairs covered in a chintz ivory material. The toss pillows were the palest mint green she had ever seen. The same pale mint was picked up in the stripe on the small settee that separated the chairs. The oval coffee table had inlaid ivory carvings. Chocolates and hard candies lay in baccarat crystal dishes on the table. Emily's eyes shifted to the second sitting area. It was larger, more masculine. It included dark burgundy leather chairs with a navy leather couch and deep cherry accents, as well as oil paintings of hunting dogs hanging over the couch.

Emily absorbed all of the surroundings quickly as she always did when summing up someone. She took in details others would miss. Emily never missed details— especially expensive ones. The one thing missing in this office was anything personal. Only a simple, yet elegant, silver frame of an older woman sat on the desk. She was striking, but Emily didn't know if the picture was old or new. The woman looked to be in her 50s, and was very beautiful.

She thought Mr. Shane must be her husband, and that he could be anywhere from fifty to a hundred years old. There were no pictures of children anywhere in the office. Just the silver-framed photograph of the woman and a huge oil painting of a man. His eyes were the softest gray, and Emily found herself staring at them. She believed them to be kind and gentle eyes. Was that Marcus Shane?

The young woman was speaking to her and Emily had to rejoin the conversation. "I'm sorry. What did you say?"

The secretary studied Emily before speaking. "I said, Mr. Shane will join you in just a moment. Are you sure I can't get anything for you?"

"No, nothing at all, but thank you." Emily stood quietly and calmly and very at ease in the middle of the room. She let her eyes drift from piece to piece. Emily studied the artwork, the figurines that graced the finely carved tables. She noticed the Waterford crystal ashtrays, the sterling silver coffee server, the fresh lilacs and roses in their own large crystal vases.

She breathed deeply, and then heard a man clear his throat. As she turned, Emily saw Marcus Shane standing in the doorway, which must have led to a private study and bathroom area. It was obvious that he had been watching her.

Marcus Shane was mid-thirties, maybe older, she guessed, with boyish good looks. His trim body was tanned, and he emanated so much charisma that Emily thought she could actually see it radiate from his body. When he smiled at her, and proffered his arm for her to take a seat, Emily found herself blushing, probably for the first time in a long while. Surprisingly, it was the same feeling she had felt when she had first met Eric, who was supposedly the purported love of her life. Emily shuddered at the thought.

Marcus Shane took it as a personal affront that she didn't like him or his elegant suite of offices, and was taken aback. Emily noticed this immediately. She smiled sheepishly as she extended her hand to him.

"Hello, Mr. Shane. I'm Emily Anderson Blake, and I love your offices. They are beautifully adorned. You chose a wise and creative and very talented interior designer. Please excuse any rudeness on my part. I have, quite frankly, been under a lot of stress. I am here to ask your help in obtaining a divorce."

# Chapter Fifteen

MARCUS SHANE COULDN'T concentrate. He couldn't remember a single time when it had happened before. He was absolutely mesmerized by the lovely creature sitting before him.

He studied her facial features carefully. He watched intently as her lips curved ever so slightly upward at their corners. He noticed the softness of her beautiful pale golden hair and how it actually radiated silkiness as the fragile tendrils framed her luminescent, delicate skin.

Marcus studied the almost indiscernible lines beginning to tug at the edges of her lovely but sad eyes. Her eyes. What color would one call them? The color of the sea? The color of the sky on a brilliant October day? The color of a gem catching the light from the sun? Her eyes are looking into my soul. They are pleading with me. Yes, pleading, he thought.

Emily continued to speak, but Marcus was lost in her, rather than her words. He was treading unfamiliar territory, for Marcus was smitten.

How could anyone, any man in his right mind, want to hurt this woman child? She still had an edge of vulnerability, although she would never have thought that herself, Marcus mused.

No, in her mind she was strong, and she was a fighter. She believed she was prepared to do battle against a man that had torched her soul. Well, Marcus knew men, too. He knew that most of them covered their ass pretty well these days. This Eric Blake sounded as if he were well versed in how to set up a woman, take her for everything, and leave her standing at the altar, so to speak.

Seeing she had only been married less than a year, he could try to seek an annulment for her. In fact, that was exactly what he would recommend. She was still childish about the situation and it was because of her pain that she wanted revenge. She would come around though. They usually did. Fighting men such as Eric was never a win-win situation.

Marcus listened to the nightmarish tale of the hospital stay and her return to the apartment, where she found herself locked out and all of her possessions gone. My God, he thought, this had only been twenty four hours ago. How was this woman sitting before him, recollecting all of these insipid details in a precise manner and not totally breaking down and falling completely apart in a fit of sobs? That is how most women would react.

Marcus thought Emily might like, or even need, a shoulder to cry on. She just wasn't ready to cry yet. But when she was, he knew he damn well wanted to be that shoulder.

Emily told Marcus Shane everything. The floodgate of truth she had held closed for so long opened up and she spouted every single facet of her life she could bare to reveal.

She told him of her family, which Eric never knew about. She told him where she grew up. She told him about her high school years. She told him about her work. For some reason, she didn't want to leave this man's office. She wanted to talk to him all day. She felt safe. She was tired of having secrets, and if this Marcus Shane was going to truly help her, he needed to know everything. So she complied. That is, as best as Emily knew how to comply. For so long, her life had been such a series of secrets and a series of denials that Emily wasn't sure where to start or stop.

"Where will you stay now that you don't have your apartment any longer, Mrs. Blake?" Emily had already covered this base. She spoke with some feeling of accomplishment.

"I've already called my old roommates, as well as the company. They were very kind. Fortunately for me, no one has been assigned to the place, so I'll just move right back into my old room."

Marcus rose, signaling that the meeting had come to an end. He knew he had taken more time with her than he generally took with three new clients. For some reason, it hadn't mattered to Marcus. Time wasn't important. This woman was.

"I'll check out your investments, your bank statements, try to get a hold on his accounts as well, his employer, and what not. Please leave me your number and I will call you in a few days. That is if you are in town. If you know your flight schedule, perhaps you could leave it with my secretary. I think that would be very helpful." Marcus tried to sound as nonchalant as possible, but schoolboy uneasiness seemed to creep into his voice. Emily didn't notice because she was too absorbed in thinking that she had found someone who could really help her. She just thanked her lucky stars she'd found the right attorney. The Eric Blake's of the world couldn't always win. Eric needed to learn that he couldn't spit on her, kill her baby, and then just simply walk away. Disappear into the night, leaving her high and dry. Leaving like a cold wind that whips through, chilling you to the bone, and leaving all in its wake dampened and weakened.

As she stepped outside of the plush offices, she felt lighter, more buoyant than when she had arrived. She actually felt fine. The only thing she wanted to do was to forget the last eighteen months of her life. Then her lower lip began to tremble as she realized what had just happened.

"My God," she whispered. "Here I stand again, wanting to forget a part of my life. If I keep this up, I won't have any part I want to remember."

She shook her head as a cool breeze ruffled her skirt. She had to smile, even if she was on the verge of tears. She wiped them away and dared them to fall as they threatened. Things certainly couldn't get any worse. She had been to hell and back. She was back. Emily was a fighter and she knew it. Today is the first day of the rest of your life she told herself. I better start living it and enjoying it.

Marcus Shane's image flashed before her. "My God, Emily, you aren't even divorced yet and here you are thinking of another man!" she chided herself. Little did she know that Marcus Shane at that very moment couldn't think of anything else but her as well.

# Chapter Sixteen

WHEN THE TELEPHONE RANG exactly one week after her meeting with Marcus Shane, Emily thought little of it. She had flown her usual route, and had been home exactly two hours, and was preparing a much anticipated and needed bath, filled with scented rose petals. The candles were already lit and their sweet fragrance filled the small room. The telephone was more of an annoyance than anything else right now. She just wanted to soak, redo her nails, lather her body in oils, and sleep. She wanted to sleep for three days, but she answered the ringing machine anyhow.

"Hello, Mrs. Blake? This is Marcus Shane. Have I caught you at a bad time?"

Emily swallowed hard to keep her voice from cracking. More than once over the past week he had entered her thoughts. "No, of course not. You haven't intruded upon a thing."

Quickly forgotten was the lovely treasured warm bath awaiting her, the candles all aglow, and the needed and wished for sleep. She forgot about the world. She was talking to Marcus Shane and she was hanging onto every word.

"Mrs. Blake, my news isn't good. Now, I know it isn't at all in the ordinary process of things, but instead of coming to my office in the morning, or tomorrow afternoon, I would like to meet with you. I guess what I'm trying to say and still sound professional saying it is, will you have dinner with me tonight? I would like to discuss your case outside of the office."

There, thought Marcus. I got it out. Why did this woman bring out a sudden shyness in him? He definitely wasn't shy. He could have any woman he wanted. He just hadn't wanted any of them. But that had changed when Emily Blake had walked into his office. His news was bad. Very bad. He didn't want her to have to face it alone. He wanted to be there, not only as her attorney, but as a friend, too.

"Why, dinner would be absolutely wonderful, Mr. Shane."

Emily immediately went into high gear. She only had four hours before her dinner "date," and it was already becoming the social event of her life, she thought. She was on her fifth outfit and still couldn't decide what to wear. Why was she acting like this, and why did she care? If she could answer those two questions, she thought wearily, she could bring peace to her inner self.

"Oh, Emily, just pick something!"

Emily picked up the first outfit she had tried on. A lovely sea foam green suit. She always wore it with a blouse the color of creamy butter. Every time she had it on, Emily knew eyes were drawn to her. The two colors together seemed to bring out the color of her hair and the color of her eyes at the same time. Yes. Perfect. She wondered why she had ever doubted her first choice in the first place.

Just dressing caused Emily to be a little uneasy, although she wasn't sure why. Marcus Shane was her attorney. What news could possibly be worse than the life she had just lived?

No. No matter what the "bad news" was, Emily could handle it and so could Marcus Shane. She was sure of it.

Reassessing her image one final time in the gold leafed mirror, Emily studied her reflection. She lifted her fingers and touched the image staring back at her. "Let's go. We can do this."


MARCUS SHANE WATCHED EMILY enter the restaurant. She was even more gorgeous than he had remembered. She held her head regally. She had class. She had style. She knew what to do and when to do it. She was a lady. That was it. She might have had a humble beginning in life, which also suited him just fine, but she had carved and created herself into a sculpted piece of art. He admired that. He thought his mother would, too.

If he was going to run for public office, he needed a wife. He needed someone just like Emily Blake. Marcus found himself laughing out loud. "Better get her an annulment before you marry her, old boy!"

He couldn't believe he was entertaining such thoughts. It would be easy enough to erase Emily's little indiscretion of bad taste and misjudgment. Eric Blake was a loser. Marcus figured he wouldn't be around much longer, especially if Marcus had anything to do with it.

Emily's world was about to come crashing down on her, but Marcus knew she would survive it all. He planned on being there to pull her up and help her recover.

SHE SAW MARCUS WALKING toward her. He was incredibly handsome. At least she knew where he worked. She knew he had a family. She knew he had never been married, and by his own choice. She wasn't ready for anything between them. She felt sure he sensed that, too. But she was ready for someone to lean on. As they were seated, Emily adjusted her chair until she was comfortable and made sure that the light hit her just right and reflected upon her more beautifully. Emily knew how to do everything to make herself look her best. She was a master at it, even if she didn't really need to do anything.

Marcus cleared his throat. "You know I could wait until after dinner to tell you everything I found out in the past week. We could have some wine, some dinner..."

Emily cut him off. "No, just tell me now. Believe me, I can handle it."

Marcus didn't want to tell her. He wanted to be able to say everything was fine. That he hadn't found anything out of the ordinary. An annulment or divorce would be clear and simple; alimony was on the way. But he couldn't.

"Emily, Eric Blake doesn't have a job, so to speak. He has connections. They are all drug connections. From my sources, I have learned that he is on the outskirts of the Philadelphia Mafia. He made some major advancement into the family but, as of about three to six months ago, he fell out of favor with them. Word has it that there is a price on his head. There is no office. There is no job. Eric Blake is a con man. He's a runner for the Mafia."

Emily felt the blood drain from her face. She would not have believed what she just heard had it not been Marcus Shane telling her.

"Well, I think I could use a drink about right now, and maybe something a little more than just wine. I think a vodka tonic with a lemon would be nice." Emily's lip began to quiver.

"Emily, that's not all. Eric has cleaned out your bank accounts, including your savings, and you have no stocks left. Your portfolio was closed out with your broker two weeks ago."

Emily knew she was going to faint. She was absolutely sure of it. She couldn't move. She couldn't cry. She couldn't do anything.

She was glad that she was sitting in a restaurant, because she knew that this would cause her to remain composed. Never in a million years would she allow herself to become unglued in public. Somehow, Marcus Shane knew that too.

The server quietly placed the drink before her. She picked up the cold, refreshing liquid and let it slide down her throat. God, it tasted good. Emily sat motionless for what seemed like an eternity.

She studied her drink, watching the perfectly cut lemon float and skim atop the crystal cut ice cubes. What a great color for a coat, Emily thought. And look how the twist in the lemon doesn't ruin the shape of the fruit, just adds to the overall look. Ok, Emily thought silently, I've lost my mind.

No not my mind, she thought, just a moment lost not wanting to face the reality of the words that had been spoken. She looked up and met Marcus Shane's eyes squarely.

"What's next?"

Marcus admired her more than anyone he knew at that very moment. Here was a woman who had just been told she had been lied to, cheated, used and abused, and every penny she had ever saved, which was quite substantial, had been legally stolen from her.

"We file for annulment. We clear the name Blake off anything you ever attached it to. We literally erase the fact that you ever knew this creep. We go about getting your stock portfolio worked back up. You go back to work. I take care of your legal troubles. This will be our little secret. You become a free woman and, after that, I get to date you.

"You see, we have a strict policy about being involved with clients, so I have made it a top priority to clear your case quickly. Emily Anderson, you deserve a lot better than what you have been dealt."

Emily actually found herself smiling, and she was even a little hungry. How? She did not know, but this man sitting across from her was just the dose of medicine she needed. She said a silent prayer of thanks and picked up the menu. The words "our little secret" turned over in her mind. Trust me, I can handle secrets, she thought silently.

# Chapter Seventeen

*A* WHIRLWIND OF TELEPHONE CALLS, long late night conversations, flying, working, dreaming, and trying to get her life in order became commonplace for Emily during the weeks that followed that first dinner with Marcus. Getting her life into order was proving to be a lot easier than she ever thought possible because of him.

He telephoned her constantly. He insisted that she call him as soon as she reached her hotel room in each city. He made sure she locked her doors and got the rest she needed. For the first time in her life, Emily felt like someone, other than her dear sweet grandmother, cared for her. "Oh, Granny, you would so like Marcus," Emily whispered.

Marcus had pulled every string he had, and he had plenty in town, to get her annulment rushed through the legal system. He had also gone the extra mile to erase Emily's past and eradicate Eric Blake from her very existence. If anyone ever checked, they would find no record of marriage, no record of apartment rentals, and no hospital records with her name on them. If Marcus Shane was anything, he was thorough.

And if anyone ever questioned anything about Emily, they would have to say it was just mistaken identity. They could search and try to uncover a connection until they were blue in the face, but Emily Blake and Emily Anderson were two different people. One happened to be a hapless soul who was taken in by a drug dealer. The other was a beautiful young woman who had never married.

Marcus sat back in his soft, overstuffed Italian leather chair. He was pleased with himself. He had taken it upon himself to make sure nothing, and he meant nothing, would ever come back to haunt Emily regarding her past. He sighed a breath of relief. Finally, all the stones unturned. All the ducks lined up in a row.

He thought of the past weeks and a slight smile tugged at the corners of his lips. He was actually excited about seeing someone, as long as that someone was Emily. The anticipation of seeing Emily and telling her all of his accomplishments on her behalf made him feel special. He didn't understand the feeling.

Tonight, he would see Emily. Not just talk into the wee hours of the night. He chuckled, thinking how they sometimes talked almost until dawn, which left each of them dragging around the next day. But they were refreshed to start the telephone conversation all over again as soon as they heard each other's voice.

Marcus Shane had a life now. He had always been very involved in his work, striving for the excellence his mother demanded, and one day this would amount to running for a coveted office in the state legislature, or congress. But, in order to succeed at that, he needed a woman by his side. Finally, he had found her, or she had found him. It didn't matter. This Sunday, Marcus planned on taking Emily to his mother's house for the formal introduction.

# Chapter Eighteen

AS THEY DROVE UP THE LONG, winding driveway, Emily gave Marcus a sideways glance. He looked comfortable and handsome. He sensed her staring at him.

"Are you nervous?"

Emily smiled easily at his observation. "Not really nervous. I guess I feel like I'm getting ready to be inspected and I just hope I pass the inspection."

Marcus laughed. "How could you possibly not pass an inspection? You are beautiful. You are young. You have never been married."

Emily shot him a look of concern. Marcus reached into his pocket and handed her an envelope. Emily opened it gingerly. Contained inside were the annulment documents for one Emily Anderson, formally of Kentucky. "But I'm from Tennessee," Emily said.

"I know you are. The Emily Anderson that married Eric Blake was from Kentucky. I guess a real coincidence, but hey, it happened."

Emily reached her hand over and placed it on his. "Thank you," she said softly.

"Emily, it's over dear. You can stop worrying. As far as the paper trail goes, it goes nowhere. Sure, there will be some people who know about Eric. But from what you say, not many. Plus, those people aren't important. You are free and clear. And by the way, you do have stocks and your portfolio is looking rather good." Emily's mouth flew open. "What on earth are you talking about? You told me Eric…"

Marcus smiled and waved his hand for her to be quiet. "Emily, I couldn't have my mother looking into your background and discover you were penniless. So, I just helped you out a bit. Hey, any attorney worth his salt would have done it for you."

Emily sat in silence. She was stunned, and she didn't know if she liked what he had done. Changing her past and her identity for the good was one thing, but to put money in her name to make it look like she had more than she did was another. She got ready to protest when they pulled to a stop in front of the large colonial home.

"Your mother certainly has a beautiful home, Marcus," Emily said, almost too curtly.

Marcus stroked her beautiful face tenderly. "It's okay, Em. Please don't be angry with me. I just want to help you. I know it's quick, but I care for you. I care deeply. I want to take care of you. I love my mother, but she can be a real pain sometimes. I don't want her causing you any problems."

Marcus gently brushed his lips across her cheek, and then got out of the car and headed around to open her door. Under her breath, Emily muttered, "Cause me any problems. More like cause you any problems."


THE SHANE MANSION WAS enormous. The stately brick and white columns did not do justice to the grandeur of the interior. The mansion was a replica of the Southern homes Emily had only seen from a distance over the years and never entered.

When the rotund maid waddled forward, her genuine smile of happiness to see Marcus momentarily made Emily forget that she was a little angry with him.

"Oh my my, Marcus. You have outdone yourself this time. Why, this happens to be the most beautiful girl you've brought here all week," she teased.

"Now Mattie, she'll up and leave if you put thoughts like that in her head." The two obviously liked each other a great deal. Mattie had been with Marcus's family for more than thirty years. He loved her and she him. She wrapped her big arms around him and gave him a hug.

"Now, you two just go right on into the parlor. Your mother has been pacing the floor waiting on this visit. Dinner will be in one hour."

She turned to Emily. "Don't you worry one bit, Missy. You are a beautiful woman and you look like you just stepped off one of those pages from one of Mrs. Shane's magazines. She will be pleased with you. So, you go in there and you be yourself." With that said, Mattie turned and waddled back toward the kitchen.

Emily and Marcus burst out laughing. "Well, Mattie never was one to mince words. She's been with us most of my life. She knows me and she knows my mother. So trust her. I know I do," Marcus said, in an almost too melancholy fashion.

Mrs. Abigail Shane was a statuesque woman of sixty-five. Her hair was light ash blonde and her figure trim. She was a good two inches taller than Emily. Emily envisioned that the woman loved being tall so she could always look down on people. Emily straightened her shoulders. She knew when someone was accessing her, and she was being raked over the coals right now, not just observed.

Emily was glad she had chosen her cream Chanel suit. Her wedding dress. The thought gave Emily a boost of confidence. She already had one up on this lady and the woman didn't even know it. Yes, this is the suit I wore when I married a drug dealer who stole everything from me. Emily felt a little giddy. She smiled, revealing nothing as she extended her hand.

"It is so very lovely to meet you. I thank you for inviting me into your beautiful home."

Mrs. Shane proffered her hand and lightly shook Emily's. "My dear, any friend of Marcus's is indeed welcome in my home. And such a lovely creature at that," enthused Mrs. Shane.

Emily was sure she heard sarcasm in the voice, but Marcus just beamed with pride. He was oblivious to what his mother was saying or doing. He thought things were going swimmingly, while Emily knew the mother was already building up a dislike for her.

The hour before dinner dragged painfully by. Each minute felt like an hour. They chatted briefly of politics, touched on books each had read lately, the summer heat, the new transportation system, and what it was like to fly for a living and travel to different places and stay in "hotel" rooms all alone in strange cities.

Yes, Emily got the message. Marcus did not. Emily let out a huge breath of relief when good-byes were said all around. Mrs. Shane shook her hand.

"Please come back and visit sometime, Emily. You are a remarkable girl with so many exciting stories to tell."

Emily nodded. "I'd love that, Mrs. Shane. I really would." As Emily turned to leave, Mattie eased just close enough for Emily to hear her and no one else, "Don't you let her bother you. She doesn't think anyone is good enough for that son of hers. But you held your own just fine. In time, you'll win her over. Just don't you fret over the likes of Mrs. Shane."

With that said, Mattie handed Emily her purse and they walked down the steps, taking in the colorful impatiens that graced the enormous urns on the verandah and stone steps.

Emily slid into the car and leaned her head against the supple leather. Marcus shut his door and looked over at her and smiled.

"That went well. I am so glad my mother liked you. You were marvelous, my dear. I am so proud of you. My mother can be difficult at times, but you handled her like an old pro." He leaned over and kissed her, first gently, and then more urgently. Emily was taken aback, but she returned his kiss. She liked it more than she wanted to.

## ▪ Ten Months Later ▪

ABIGAIL SHANE LAID THE newspaper down with a disgusting grunt. "I just cannot believe Marcus is marrying some girl from Tennessee who flies for a living. Why, she is from working class, lower income people. I just don't think this will bode well with the voters."

Pausing, she thought about what she had just said. "Of course, we will just have to turn it to our advantage. We could illustrate how she rose above all that, and how she understands the plight of the poor, perhaps. Well, maybe she can be an asset. She certainly has done well for herself."

Mattie looked on, agreeing with every word. "I know one thing, Mrs. Shane. You sure have put together the wedding of the century. I know Miss Emily is as proud of you as any daughter would ever be." Mattie always knew how to settle Mrs. Shane down.

"Yes, she does seem pleased. Of course, who wouldn't? We have spared no expense."

That, of course, was almost an understatement. Abigail Shane had thrown herself into planning the wedding, much to Emily's chagrin. She would have liked to have been more involved.

She had decided to work until three months before the wedding, at which point she could become actively involved. By the time she quit the airline, everything was finished, except for the wedding itself.

Emily had provided only a few names. Her mother and father were flying in from Tennessee, and that was all the family she had asked to come. Emily had sent them airline tickets weeks ago.

Marcus had made reservations at one of the nicer downtown hotels for them. When Emily thought about it, she realized it would probably be the first time either had ever stayed in something other than a trailer park, RV center, or drive up motel.

If Emily had her wishes, she wouldn't have invited her parents. She hadn't seen or spoken with them since she had walked out of their house more than four years earlier. She didn't care to see or speak with them now. But Marcus had said that to omit them would be drawing attention to them. So, they made the list. Now, they would be arriving soon.

Emily's feelings vacillated between dread and excitement. I wonder if they've aged. I wonder if they will think I look different. She looked around the room filled with new clothes. She certainly felt different. Maybe seeing her parents wasn't such a bad idea after all. In fact, it might even be nice to have someone in her corner for a change.

But right this moment Emily had more important things to do. She wanted to try her dress on one more time and physically go over each inch of it to make sure it was perfect.

Carefully, she lifted the treasure out of its long padded box.

Emily believed that floating on air must feel exactly the same way she felt at this precise moment. Timidly, she let her long slender fingers gracefully trace over the satin garment. Thousands of tiny seed pearls, each hand sewn with painstaking precision, stared back at her. She allowed herself to touch each and every single part of the dress. This dress was Cinderella's gown and, finally, she was playing the role of Cinderella.

The dress had been designed for Emily. She had gone, at Mrs. Shane's insistence, to her personal dressmaker. Emily would have preferred to shop the streets of New York for a dress, or even hire her own handpicked designer, but if the truth were known, she actually hadn't had the time. This way Mrs. Shane thought she had won a tremendous battle, when in reality, Emily hadn't even fought that fight.

But it had turned out to be a major inconvenience in the long run. Emily had eight fittings to date. The elder Mrs. Shane would have preferred to have been at each one of them, forcing her input and opinion on the design and creation of the dress. But Emily had always managed to stay one step ahead of her. She scheduled fittings when she knew Abigail couldn't possibly attend.

On the evening of her Club Social, Emily had held a three hour fitting, carefully selecting each bead and the exact placement and flow of the beads. Emily wanted spectacular. She didn't want simple. She didn't want extravagant. She wanted rich, luxurious, elegance beyond words. She wanted the congregation to gasp in sheer pleasure at the sight of her when she entered the church and began her ascent down the aisle.

The train on the dress trailed ten feet. Each folded panel was encrusted with seed pearls and Italian antique lace, which had caused Emily to squeal in delight just as a child might when first shown a desired toy. The lace alone had increased the cost of the dress tenfold, but Emily didn't care.

Marcus had made it very clear that she was to spare absolutely no expense on the dress, on herself, on her new wardrobe, and on the wedding. Emily knew exactly how to spend money. She would make Marcus a perfect wife. Not a showy one, just one with pure class, who would be regally elegant at every function, every dinner, and every outing.

The dress fit like a glove, clinging to her slender frame. Emily carefully lifted the veil from its large padded box. She cocked her head from side to side, studying her reflection in the long mirror. She had decided to wear her hair upswept with tendrils framing her face. The veil and flowing netting and lace reached the ground. Emily was going to look stunning. She almost took her own breath away.

# Chapter Nineteen

*A*BIGAIL SHANE WAS ON THE verge of pulling off the biggest social event of the entire season. Probably of the entire year. She was extremely pleased with herself, and it showed.

Meticulously she leafed through the morning papers. The rehearsal dinner had made all of them. A photo of the smiling, radiant couple, looking lovingly into each other's eyes, stared back at her from the dining room table where she was taking her morning coffee.

Perhaps Emily would be an asset after all. She was smart, easy to control, loved her son, and had good taste. She hated to admit it, and she would never publicly do so, but the pale pink Oscar de la Renta evening gown Emily had selected made her look like a princess.

She smiled, remembering her own wedding so many years before. It had not been the grand affair that her son's would be. But it had still carried its own charm. Of course, Marcus's father had yet to make his fortune in the oil industry at that time. They were just young lovers setting out on life's adventures.

Abigail always knew that Marcus Senior would succeed. She prided herself in helping him reach the top. She made him work harder, and for longer hours. She entertained the right social circles, spreading just a hint of stories here and there with necessary information to the right people. It had not taken long for Marcus Senior to rise in the ranks of the oil company, and he eventually took over the helm outright by buying out the corporate leaders. He had died ten years ago of a massive heart attack. Abigail and Marcus, Jr. had been left with millions of hard earned dollars.

At the same moment Abigail Shane thought of her wedding day, Emily studied her own image in the morning paper. She looked happy. Marcus looked happy. Even his mother looked happy. Emily shook her head. She just couldn't believe it was all happening to her.

"Well, this morning is no different than any other! Ha!" Emily said to herself playfully. This day is like no other in the world.

"My wedding day. Today is my Wedding Day," she yelled to no one in particular. She suddenly realized she was truly a bundle of nerves.

Emily thought of her soon to be mother-in-law. The woman was a social structure all to herself. Emily found that she was a shade jealous of how calm, cool, and collected Abigail Shane had been throughout the many wedding parties and social functions, and especially the rehearsal dinner the previous night.

Emily's parents had arrived the day before and, although it had been awkward, they had exchanged the perfunctory hugs and kisses and small talk before Emily had whisked them safely to the hotel where new clothes awaited each of them.

They knew Emily was probably embarrassed by them. They were small town folks, but they were not stupid. Her father picked up his new suit, which had just been delivered to him from the dry cleaners. Emily had gone to special lengths to pick out a stunning tuxedo for her father. But right now, as she watched him caress the soft fabric, she found herself feeling pity for him because of her actions. She could see that perhaps she had chipped a little bit of pride away from him by forcing him to accept her gift of nice clothing.

"You know, Emily," her father said, "I brought my Sunday suit. Your mother brought something beautiful, too. You didn't have to spend your hard earned money on clothes for us. Your mother has worked very hard on sewing a new dress since the day you called telling us about the wedding. I think you would have been real proud of her in that dress. I mean, I appreciate your kindness, but her dress is just as nice as this fancy store bought one."

Emily felt her resolve waiver, but she thought of Marcus's mother's glaring and condescending eyes.

"Well, Dad, I just thought you deserved some new clothes. I know it was a long trip for you and, well, you might not have known about the finicky weather we have here in Seattle. I just wanted to give you a gift, that's all."

Emily knew that wasn't all, and so did her father. He just nodded and took his wife's hand. Emily's mother said very little.

"You look real pretty, Emily. It seems like life has been real good to ya since ya left Sevierville. Your Marcus fellow sounds like a nice young man, and I'm happy you have found love. I wish you much happiness. Your father and I brought you this."

Her mother extended her hand, and in it was a small box wrapped in plain gold paper and tied with a yellow ribbon. Emily took the small package with trembling hands. She had not figured on such an emotional reunion with her parents. She had successfully forgotten their existence for the past four years. She had successfully forgotten all the hardships, all the things she had not liked about her past life in Sevierville.

But had they been bad parents? Did she hate her mother because she never did anything about her own brothers? But how could she do something about a situation she never knew happened? Did she hate her because she had slept too hard that fateful night? Did she hate her father because he hadn't come home in time to save her?

She looked up at these two people she had divorced herself from years ago. She had withdrawn herself from them more than ten years ago on that cold December night.

But here they were, unaware of anything in her life other than what had happened on the surface. Her mother had sewn her clothes and tried very hard to give her what she could. Her father had worked every day of his life at the chair factory since Emily could remember. She was glad they were here now as she slowly unwrapped the package.

As Emily tore away the outer gold foil wrapping, a beautiful delicate blue box was revealed. A lump rose in her throat. She didn't want to cry. She didn't want to care. Slowly, and with an anticipation she hadn't experienced in a long time, she carefully lifted the lid of the box. Emily felt the tears sting her eyes. She didn't understand.

"It was your grandmother's," her mother said. "She got it on her wedding day. I got it on mine. I never wore it 'cause it was just too special, and probably the nicest thing I ever owned in my whole life, except for the little gold band your Daddy gave me. We always knew you'd wear it one day. You have a lot of fine jewelry, and it might not be fancy enough for you to wear, but we still wanted ya to have it. I know your grandma would like that."

Emily was speechless. The tears stained her face and her guard was completely gone. She lowered herself to the hotel bed. She didn't like how she felt. Here she had a two carat diamond on her finger, a solid gold watch, a bracelet laced with diamonds on her wrist, and huge diamond earrings that decorated each earlobe. But the locket Emily held in her hands was more valuable to her than all of these pieces put together. She didn't think her parents would believe her.

She studied the locket carefully. It was the size of a quarter. The deeply engraved etchings formed roses and small leaves. More of a vine wrapping around the roses, Emily thought. In the middle of the gold treasure was a pinpoint-sized diamond. Emily carefully moved the clasp opening it. Inside were three beautifully scripted words: "To My Love."

Emily swallowed hard. She let her tears slide down her cheeks. Her voice was raw with emotion as she tried to speak. "Thank you. This is the most precious gift I have ever received. I will always treasure it."

Emily rose and left her parents in their lonely hotel room. She walked quickly to her own room and stopped in front of the large mirror, placing the locket around her neck.

That had been last night, and now as Emily studied her own image in the paper, she absentmindedly reached for the locket around her neck. Marcus had immediately noticed it when she had seen him before dressing for the rehearsal dinner.

"It's beautiful and very attractive. Quite a nice sentimental piece, but I dare say, you of all people, with your expert fashion sense, know it will never do with your evening gown." Emily had started to protest that she had to wear it because of the sentimental reason. But then Mrs. Shane had ever so politely added her two cents.

"Oh, Emily. My oh my. What a nice little locket. Now, that will be great with your casual attire. Tonight, I thought you might just like to borrow the diamond choker my dear Marcus gave me so many years ago."

She had probably bought the choker for herself, or ripped it off some poor corporate head's wife in one of the many hostile company takeovers, Emily thought. The old woman was clever. She certainly knew how to manipulate a situation. How could Emily say no and turn one sentimental piece down for another more appropriate sentimental piece. Emily had gently stroked the locket and allowed Marcus to slip it off of her neck. Abigail had screamed at the young maid to bring Emily the diamond choker.

Emily had finally caved in and agreed that she was being silly. She must look her best for the rehearsal dinner. She had placed the treasured necklace back in its box and worn the diamond choker instead.

Now, as she sat at the breakfast table of her hotel suite, she toyed with the necklace she had put on as soon as she had returned last night. Her parents had noticed she had not worn the necklace. She had seen the disappointment in their faces, but they said not a word.

But today was her wedding day and she would wear the locket and she would probably wear it from that day forward. She decided it would become her signature piece. Casual attire or not. She touched it lightly and thought of her grandmother.

The necklace gave her strength. The light tapping on the door startled her. "Just a minute," Emily said. She opened her door and her mother stood there smiling.

"Good morning," her mother said. "Thought you might need some help on your wedding day."

Emily smiled. "Yes, that would be great. I have my stylist coming at noon, and a manicurist at two. Also, I have a wardrobe consultant coming by at two, so you can help her out. Why don't we order room service? I could use a little bite. Where's dad?" Emily asked, realizing that her parents were most likely very scared in such a big city and also very bored with nothing to do.

"Oh, he decided to stroll the streets. You know your father, he likes to explore."

"No, I didn't know that about him." Emily said sadly.

"Well, it's a good thing you are having an evening wedding. This way you have all day to get prepared, and if you get cold feet, you have a full day to run," her mother laughed. "I like your locket. It looks real pretty on that long swan's neck of yours."

Emily clutched the necklace, "I love the necklace. Thank you. I wanted to wear it last night but…"

Her mother stopped her from speaking. "Emily, I guess we just do what we gotta do. Don't you fret. I'll stay here with you for a few hours, and then go get myself all ready. We have an early flight back home tomorrow. I'm glad you planned it liked that. You know your Daddy can't take too much time off. I got a full week off. I've just been so excited telling everybody about you getting married. We put it in the Sevierville Times, but I had to use your old high school annual picture. I hope you don't mind. You're much prettier now. All grown up and mature. A real woman. You look just like a princess. Your grandma sure would be happy for you. I bet she is looking down on you right now, just a smilin'."

Emily liked to think that. She often thought her grandmother was watching over her. She felt a closer connection to her now more than ever as she tenderly stroked the locket.

# Chapter Twenty

EMILY STOOD IN THE VESTIBULE CLINGING to her father's arm. She could feel a slight tremor coursing through his body. She swallowed hard, trying to make the lump in her throat disappear. She had neglected, forgotten, and forsaken her parents for close to four years. Yet, here was her father, trying not to cry as he walked her down the aisle.

Her parents, along with the six hundred other assembled guests, didn't know this was Emily's second trip down an aisle. Hopefully, they never would. Emily's large azure eyes looked deeply into her father's, and she nodded, indicating that she was ready to proceed.

Marcus's mother had politely and carefully selected six bridesmaids for Emily, since she wasn't like most young women with hordes of friends. She didn't have a best friend to serve as maid of honor. The only person she had considered was Karen, her old apartment manager. But Emily knew Karen held too many secrets concerning her past. One slip and her world would be tainted, or rather, Marcus's world would be tainted with all of those stains he had so carefully cleaned up and polished.

She also hadn't wanted anyone from the airline to attend, since she had left her job months ago, breaking off all contact with the other girls. Marcus had said it would be best to erase whatever memories she could from their mind.

Most would not be permanent residents of the Seattle area as she would be, and the nauseating circumstances of her past mistake with Eric could be forgotten.

For those with a memory, Marcus had a sure and ready answer. They were never officially wed. She had a brief fling with him and, not wanting to seem wanton, had told her co-workers she was married. Emily didn't like this answer. She thought it made her look silly and immature. But, Marcus had insisted.

He had also assured her that Eric would soon be out of her life forever. She smiled as she remembered his words. Yes, Eric was out of her life. Now, she was entering the dazzling life of Marcus Shane.

As Marcus's first cousin waltzed down the aisle, her long, pale, yellow train cascading down her back, Emily let the tension within her be released. She took a deep breath and stood tall. Resembling a princess with a veil of shimmering pearls sparkling around her model like face, Emily took the first step down the aisle toward yet another new life and beginning.

The rising of the hordes of people made it sound as if horses would come crashing through the doors at any minute. Emily was suddenly taken aback. But, no one noticed. They were too in awe of her sublime beauty. This creature that had so captivated the most eligible bachelor in all of Seattle, and who had won the approval of the matriarch of the family. The woman who would share the same last name as the head of the family. They rose to salute a worthy woman indeed.

Emily smiled coyly, half expecting some of them to curtsey to her. Her father continued his solemn gait, counting each step and keeping his face forward, never glancing to one side or the other. Emily suddenly realized that she felt sorry for him. There was not one soul in the church he knew except himself, his wife, and his daughter.

He had no one to look to and wink, as if saying, "Look, this is my little girl getting married." Instead, he was in the beautiful tuxedo Emily had rented for him, walking in shoes that didn't belong to him, and staring ahead to a man he would give his daughter to, whether he liked it or not.

As they reached the end of the aisle, Emily and her father stopped. The Most Reverend Bishop Emerson Franks, in his deep resonant voice began. "Dearly beloved, we are gathered here on this day to join this man and this woman in holy matrimony. Who shall stand to give this woman to this man?" With that, Emily's father stepped back one step—a move that was well rehearsed the night before—and he proffered Emily's hand to Marcus.

"Her mother and I do." Her father turned, rather uneasily, and faced the large crowd momentarily, before shifting his gaze to his wife. He walked at a fast clip and sat in the seat next to her as beads of sweat broke upon his brow. Marjorie gently laid her hand over his shaking one.

Emily was nervous. She had not expected to be so. The flowers, the enormity of the church, the hundreds of eyes upon her, and the man standing beside her exuded so much power it was frightening.

In a trance like state she said all the right things, bowed at the appropriate times, closed her eyes during the prayers, and held her hand out without the slightest tremble as the slender band of platinum was slipped upon the third finger of her left hand.

She smiled into Marcus's eyes. It was a blur, but she clearly heard Bishop Franks saying, "I now pronounce you man and wife."

Emily tilted her head slightly as Marcus slowly and gently, and with great care, lifted her veil. He leaned close to her and brushed her lips ever so lightly. It was over. It was official. She was Mrs. Marcus Shane. As she turned to face the church, she was met with smiling faces, flowers, music, her parents, and a feeling of warmth and love. Emily felt pure and, most of all, she felt like she had a future.

Emily let her mind wander only fleetingly to her "other" wedding, the one that was in hushed tones with no one in attendance. She remembered how they walked out of the church very quickly, as if they were in hiding.

Now, six hundred well wishers stood before her, all beaming with joy. Sheer happiness raced through her body. The electricity of her new life was bringing her closer and closer to the euphoric feeling that nothing could stop her now.

Bolstered by an incredible dose of self worth, pride, and confidence, Emily returned the admiring crowd's smile and floated down the aisle with Marcus on her arm. She looked at her mother and father and felt a pure love for them she had not experienced since she was a child. Without rehearsal or forethought, she stopped and gently kissed her father's cheek and hugged her mother. If Marcus was upset by this unexpected or unchoreographed move, he didn't bring it to anyone's attention. She looked at him and again slipped her arm through his.

Continuing down the aisle, Emily nodded and smiled and mouthed "thank you" as if she had done this a thousand times and being in the midst of a crowd was nothing more than attending an afternoon tea. Mrs. Marcus Shane, Sr. did not miss this natural flow of emotion emanating from Emily. She was a natural with crowds. She knew how to work one and work one well. She was beautiful on her son's arm. She noticed how Emily blended and flowed with ease with the masses. Yes, Mrs. Marcus Shane, Sr. was very pleased. She had indeed found Marcus a good wife after all.


EMILY STRETCHED HER BACK, AND then grabbed the sun tanning lotion from the linen bag she had brought to the pool. A young man appeared by her side, and said, "May I get you another blended lemonade, Madame?"

Emily cocked her head and tilted her oversized brimmed hat to the side. "Thanks. That would be lovely. This time, please put fresh strawberries in it, too." The young boy nodded and disappeared.

Emily liked this service. She had fit into it like a glove. It hadn't even taken her a day to disassociate herself from the hired help and the maids and the caterers.

"They are paid handsomely. They work for you. They are not your 'buddies.' They are your employees. I hope that is clear," Marcus had said. He had been almost stern with her.

The maid in their condo was young and efficient. She had unpacked Emily's beautiful new clothes with the utmost care. She had pressed everything, including her undergarments. Emily was living a fairy tale, and this was the best honeymoon any princess could ever wish for.

Emily reached for the latest Women's Wear Daily issue and began to flip through it. She wondered where Marcus was. He had said he would play golf until three and then join her poolside. She had only been out for forty-five minutes, not wanting to catch the hottest rays of the day. Emily knew she had to protect her skin. She intended to do so.

An envelope slipped from the magazine. Emily lifted it from the ground. She looked around. The envelope was addressed to her and was in Marcus's handwriting. She smiled a girlish smile.

"Love letters already."

She gleefully tore into the envelope, but exercised caution so as to not tear anything. Inside was a newspaper clipping. Emily put her hand to her mouth to stop her gasp.

The bold headline jumped out at her.

## "YOUNG DRUG LORD FOUND DEAD IN SEATTLE ALLY"

Eric's name stared out at her. Was this a sick joke? Eric was dead. Emily quickly scanned the article, her mouth dry. "Eric Land, also know as Eric Blake, Richard Blake and last known as Eric Anderson...."

Emily shook her head from side to side in disbelief as she read on. "He even stole my name?"

The article stated that he had never been to Seattle before. This was his first big job with an offshoot of a New York mob family, and he had been assigned, so the government said, to start new projects on the West Coast. Evidently, his first stop in town was the wrong one.

Emily felt sick to her stomach. She couldn't read anymore. She swung her legs over her chair and hurriedly put her belongings back in the large linen designer bag. The boy approached with her lemonade. She thanked him and laid it beside her as she finished throwing things into her bag. Clutching the envelope tightly to her chest, she practically ran to the penthouse.

When she put her key into the lock, it turned easily. The maid greeted her immediately, taking her things. Emily went to her room where fresh clothes were laid out on the bed.

"When you are finished undressing, I will take your swimwear, Madame. Would you like some fresh fruit or juice?"

Emily turned and stopped. "No, I would like a vodka tonic on the rocks with a twist of lemon."

She turned around and totally dismissed the young maid. Marcus heard Emily return to the condo. He had listened to her order a drink.

He paused before entering the master bedroom.

"Hello my love, did you have a good swim? I was getting ready to come join you," he said simply, with a nonchalant attitude.

"Marcus, what is the meaning of this?" Emily stated, waving the envelope in the air.

Marcus shook his head and raised his shoulders, studying her. "I don't know what you mean. What is the meaning? It means we do not have to worry about that monster ever bothering you again. He is dead and out of your life forever."

The words ripped through Emily. They were thunderbolts. Run, Emily. Run. That is what her mind was telling her. She had heard those words before.

"He will be out of your life forever." The exact promise Marcus had made to her only weeks ago. And now Eric was out of her life forever. He was dead.

"Did you have anything to do with his death? Did you cause it?"

Marcus strode the length of the room and faced her squarely. She could feel his hot breath on her as he hissed. Venom dripped from every word.

"How dare you utter such a ridiculous thing! I will never tolerate such absurd thinking on your part. Do you understand me? To actually think and then voice the thought that I might have played a part, or had a hand in something as filthy as your former lover's death, is beyond reasonable thinking. Do not ever suggest anything of that nature again. I know what you were married to before. But you are no longer associated with that type of individual. Do I make myself perfectly clear?"

Emily tried to speak. Her voice was soft and filled with hurt.

"I'm sorry Marcus. I should have known you would never do anything of the kind."

Marcus came closer and sat beside her on the bed, stroking her hair. "Emily, I thought you would be glad to know he was gone. He can't bother us. He can't hurt us. We are safe now, Emily. I love you with all of my heart. I am sorry if I broke the news to you in a foolish way. I thought you would be relieved."

With those words spoken, he gently kissed her, and all was forgotten as they laid down on the bed, escaping into each other's body. But his words lingered as she realized it wasn't her he had been protecting from Eric, but himself, and his reputation.

# Chapter Twenty-One

EMILY WATCHED AS THREE SEAGULLS vied for the same small school of fish flipping and flopping as they skimmed along the calm blue ocean before her. The last three weeks, since her storybook wedding, had soared by for Emily. She knew they would soon be only a distant memory, never forgotten and never replicated.

Having breakfast every morning on the wide open sunny deck of their lavishly appointed condominium had been only one of a dozen new life changes that Emily had quickly adapted to.

The three story condominium was one of the most beautiful on the beach in San Luis Obispo. His father had found this California paradise a few years before his death and built the complex. The building and the penthouse suite had been left to Marcus upon Marcus Sr.'s death.

As Emily looked out over the unsoiled ocean land, she wondered how long it would take before other people knew what a true jewel this place was. For now, it was slow on development. The little town had just the right amount of people.

The maids and servants stayed there and kept the place up, so it would always be ready. Marcus had a small office, and he said that they would spend at least three months of the year here.

Emily was already looking forward to her next visit. She loved her life. It couldn't get any better than this.

Before returning to Marcus's condo in the city, he had received word from his mother that they should first stop by the mansion upon their return to Seattle. Emily didn't particularly like these instructions. She wanted to get home. Her new home.

She was sure that everything had been moved from the apartment Marcus had rented her and moved into his condo. She was also sure that everything had already been placed and arranged. But still, she was excited to get to the condo, see her few belongings, and get started on rearranging the furniture, at which point she could put her personal touches to the place.

She was a new bride and everything in her life was new, and it was all good for a change. Now they had been summoned to the Queen's office, as Emily liked to think of her new mother-in-law.

What could she possible want to control now? The wedding was over. She had planned that, planned the honeymoon, bought the clothes, and picked the servants and maids. She probably had a list of children's names for them to look over in the event a blessed conception had taken place. Then Emily laughed to herself. No, of course that hadn't taken place. The Queen had not instructed them to get pregnant.

As they drove up the long winding driveway, Emily remembered how in awe she had first been when she had seen the mansion. Now it was just a large house where his mother lived. His mother took away from its beauty, from its mystic.

From the stories Emily could drag out of Marcus, it was his father who had given the place life and happiness and energy. Emily felt sad, and a sense of exclusion arose from the fact that she had never met the man so many people spoke so fondly of. At some point during each party or gathering, stories about his father's good humor, practical jokes, and goodwill were always exchanged.

He was a kind and gentle man who made sure his employees, both at his office and in his home, were well treated and looked after, including their children. In addition to being honest, he was also a hard worker.

There were tales of how he had cared for a young woman's son who had cancer and was in agonizing pain. He'd sent the child to the best doctors available and paid for the mother to stay by her son's bedside until his death. She had her job waiting for her when she was able to return to work. There were holiday stories of Santa Claus visiting the homeless and the sick. Bringing baskets of food, bags filled with toys, and money to pay the rent for dozens of families.

Marcus's father had been a truly great man. Then his wife had gained more control as he aged, and as his condition worsened.

She had taken over the reigns of the business, and the do-gooding had all but stopped. While Marcus possessed some of his father's gentle nature, he was more like his mother when it came to yearning for power and having a desire to win at all costs.

Yes, Emily thought, she would have liked to have met Marcus Senior.

Marcus rounded the corner of the sleek Jaguar and opened the door for his new bride. Emily saw the curtain slip back into place, knowing his mother had watched them drive up. As they entered the house, they were greeted, not by her, but by the butler, who took their wraps and Emily's purse. They were ushered to the drawing room, where Mrs. Shane waited patiently to be courted.

"My darlings, welcome home! You must tell me all about your wonderful vacation. I have so missed seeing you. I am glad you are back in Seattle, safe and sound. We have much to do."

Emily didn't quite know what the woman was talking about, but she had enough sense to know that she should sit there and listen to every word.

"My, the sun has done both of you wonders. You look so healthy and happy. But, I hope you are not planning on gallivanting off anytime soon again. I just can't do without you, my dear Marcus."

She smiled at Emily. Emily returned her smile, and without flinching, said, "Well, I have a lot to do to put my touches on the condo, so I don't think I will take him away for a while. But when I get ready to do so, I will be sure to give you ample notice to prepare yourself."

Emily laughed casually, trying to take the sting out of her marked words. Of course, the elder Mrs. Shane had not misunderstood the young woman. She knew she was playing a game of who controlled Marcus now.

Abigail Shane smiled secretly and sweetly within, thinking how silly and foolish this young woman must be. She tilted her head to one side as a slight smile crept across her smooth face. To think that just because Marcus was bedding her gave her some power over him. Never. I am his mother and I have controlled this man all of his life and will continue to do so.

"Well, while the two of you were away, I found the perfect wedding gift."

She handed Marcus a key and a folded slip of cream linen paper. On the paper was an address.

"What's this, Mother?" Marcus asked, truly perplexed.

"You don't think the next Congressman from our district, who has just taken a lovely new bride, can go on living in a condominium. I mean, really, Marcus. It was fine for a bachelor, but you are not a bachelor anymore!" she said with finality.

Emily sat there stunned. The woman had picked out their house? They were moving from the condo she hadn't even had the chance to put her touches on yet? She didn't even have a say as to where they were going to live? Marcus didn't have a say?

Emily looked at Marcus, expecting him to say, "Thanks, but no thanks," but those words were not uttered. Instead, he rose and hugged his mother, paying careful attention not to wrinkle her clothing or touch her hair.

"Mother, I thank you, as does Emily. But you really should have talked to us about this first."

That was it? You really should have talked to us about this first? Emily felt the room closing in on her. She thought she might pass out, but that would delight the old woman.

"Yes, Mrs. Shane. I do wish you had spoken to Marcus and me before making such a wonderful gift selection for us. I hope you won't be offended if we decline."

The old woman was mortified and Marcus was astonished.

"Why, Emily, my love. We, of course, would never decline Mother's kind gift."

Emily opened her mouth to say something, and then abruptly shut it. She just smiled. "Of course not. Where is our new home?"

Emily couldn't resist herself, although she knew in her heart she was getting ready to say something that would make Marcus angry.

"Have you had it furnished already? Or did you leave that for us to do?"

Mrs. Shane was too wise to be baited by young Emily. "Don't be silly, child. I had to leave something for you to do!"

Emily almost believed her.

THE REMAINDER OF THE DAY dragged on forever to Emily. She picked at the steak tartar on her plate and moved the asparagus from side to side.   She toyed with her salad and managed to drink the cold Chardonnay. It calmed her rattled nerves. When she first sat down, Emily had looked at the food and thought she might become ill. She quickly sipped the refreshing wine and discovered that it helped her listen to Mrs. Shane's continuing monologue on how she "discovered" the perfect house, and how much the couple was going to adore it.

Emily hated the house. She didn't even have to see it. It wasn't her house, and all the decorating and fine touches couldn't make it her house. She would be a prisoner there. Just as she was a prisoner sitting at the table listening to mother and son chatting on as if she was a mere obedient child waiting to be excused.

When the servant passed her by with the wine, Emily picked up her empty crystal glass and offered it to the young woman. Mrs. Shane stopped in mid sentence and stared at Emily.

Her voice dripping in sarcasm, disguised as motherly advice, Mrs. Shane said, "Emily, my dear. You never have to raise your glass to a server. She will gladly refill your wine glass if it is surmised that it needs filling."

Too late and too bad because the maid had already filled her glass. Emily raised the golden liquid and nodded slightly, giving Mrs. Shane a toast in the air. "I have so much to learn from you. Thank you."

Emily sipped the wine slowly. Marcus stared at her in disbelief. Had his new wife just offended his mother? The woman who had done nothing but be kind and gracious and good to her?

"Emily, are you okay, my dear?" Marcus asked.

Emily leveled her eyes at him. "I'm fine, darling. I'm exhausted from the past few weeks, and the thought of filling an entire house just, well, boggles the mind," she managed enthusiastically.

"Of course, dear, but perhaps you should slow down on the wine. It is the middle of the day," Marcus chuckled.

Every bit of the conversation that had been exchanged between Mrs. Shane and Emily had gone right over his head. Both women knew it, too. The game would be between the two of them. Emily wasn't sure she was up for the fight as she drained the wine from the crystal glass.

# Chapter Twenty-Two

EMILY FOLDED HER ARMS, HUGGING herself lightly. The house was big, almost too big. But, it did have a certain graceful flair to it. Emily chuckled to herself when she thought about how she had described it to her mother.

"It's very big, Mother," Emily had stated simply. It was actually enormous, covering ten thousand square feet and ten acres. She had to admit that the red brick against the gleaming straw white trim and lacquered black shutters added a subtle beauty to the place. The front porch was deep and wrapped around two sides of the house, verandah style, with hanging baskets overflowing with pale pink and violet colored flowers. Old world charm meets the rich and wanting to be famous, Emily mused. The driveway alone reminded her of highways back home. She wondered what her parents would think of the place, if they ever got to see it.

She doubted Marcus would want her parents around. For some reason her mother and father entered her thoughts quite often now. She would find herself, eyes closed, smiling, thinking of her father, with his trembling hands, leading her down the aisle.

She fondled the necklace around her neck. She missed them. Strange as that seemed to her, she had to acknowledge that she truly missed them. Perhaps it was simply because she felt alone more than she ever had.

Even when she was married to Eric she had not felt this alone. She had wanted to fight for something she thought was right and something she could save. And, even when she had discovered the horrible truths, and had decided that nothing was worth saving, except herself from him and the relationship, she had not felt alone.

That is because she had believed in herself and knew she was worth fighting for. Now, she always felt alone. Marcus was busy at the office twelve or more hours a day. Mrs. Shane demanded much of his attention during any precious time off he might manage, and with each passing day, Marcus became more consumed with the quest of running for office.

Most of the conversations dealt with strategies, time tables, affiliations, who to place where and when, who was contributing, and how much. Most evenings were spent either at a formal dinner or a business event. But nothing would interfere with the twice weekly dinners with his mother.

Emily sat on the floor of the library wondering how to arrange the furniture, which was to be delivered within the hour. She had taken on a workhorse approach in decorating the house. If Marcus wanted her to decorate, then she would decorate and would do so first class. No bargain hunting. No scrimping. She would decorate to the hilt and would not only make Marcus proud, but herself in the bargain.

Emily knew she possessed class of a higher category and degree than most were willing to believe or understand. She certainly hadn't been born into it, but she felt she must have been born with it. She simply knew what to do. She had turned a tiny apartment into a show place on virtually no budget. She ought to be able to make this place the Buckingham Palace on the budget Marcus had set aside.

She had politely, but quite firmly—and in her own way—insisted that Mrs. Shane refrain from stopping by, so as not to ruin the surprise, until the house was completely finished. That had been more than six months ago and the old woman had actually kept to the bargain.

Emily often wondered if the newly hired staff weren't secretly taking pictures and getting them to her. Of course, Emily also knew this was being highly paranoid on her part.

Emily rose and went to the wet bar. She let her fingers glide over the baccarat crystal glasses. The rich mahogany cabinets with beveled and stained glass were truly a work of art.

Emily had found the glass maker quite by mistake. She had been looking in the port district for an antique shop she had read about. She'd entered the warehouse and discovered an older gentleman with graying hair and thick glasses hovering over a blowtorch. Fascinated by the flame and his creation, Emily hadn't moved for several minutes.

Finally, the old man had turned the torch off and slowly turned around to face his visitor. Emily saw kindness and warmth in his dark brown eyes. She saw an artist. Their friendship had taken about five seconds to develop.

Now, the work of Solomon Shelf graced most of the rooms in some form or fashion in her home. The large stained glass window in her foyer was the focal point of the home. Rising ten feet into the air, the glass transformed the room into a waterfall cascading down smooth river rocks with rhododendrons on both sides. It would have taken most artists years to design and create these priceless pieces for her. But, she knew Solomon had worked well into each night to finish the work. In some way, he knew her better than people who had known her for years. He understood her. And he believed in her. And for that reason, he wanted to make her happy.

Emily smiled as she thought of the lovely work. This kind and talented man had helped her create a small fraction of herself in this large and cold house.

She grabbed a beautifully cut heavy tumbler from the shelf and filled it with vodka. Pouring a small amount of Bloody Mary mix into it, she sprinkled it with salt, licking her fingers. Taking her first sip, Emily shook her head and coughed. She picked up a sterling silver frame and smiled back at the people in the picture. It was a photo of Marcus and his mother on their wedding day.

"Too bad you two couldn't marry each other. I know you would have made each other very happy." Emily gave a toast to the picture, laid it face down, and drank deeply from her glass.

"Mrs. Shane, the furniture has arrived."

Emily heard the words somewhere in her dream. She was standing in a field and there were beautiful yellow daises all around her. Her grandmother was teaching her to sew. She heard her grandmother's laugh, and then the voice interrupted her again, clearing its throat.

"Mrs. Shane. The furniture has arrived and the gentleman needs your assistance.

Emily awoke with a start, realizing that she had drifted off to sleep while waiting. The maid picked up her empty glass and tossed a glance at her. Emily ignored her and just directed her gaze at the man standing in the doorway.

He was tall and handsome and had clear blue eyes. His expression bore pity for her. Emily stood up quickly and smoothed her skirt and hair.

"Good morning, I'm Mrs. Shane," Emily said, as she extended her hand.

Robby Brooks took her soft delicate hand into his strong firm one and held it a second too long.

Emily noticed his rugged good looks, his soft flannel shirt and tuffs of silky black hair peeking out from his chest. His smell was masculine, yet his eyes and face wore an expression of gentleness.

"Your home is beautiful, Mrs. Shane. The selections you have made will be perfect here."

Emily didn't know if he was making fun of her or if he was serious. She didn't know too many men, much less delivery men who knew about furniture. Emily almost stammered, but let the automatic businesswoman in her take over.

"Well, thank you. I know exactly where I want each piece. If you would please have the men bring it in here I will direct them as to where the placement should be."

Robby Brooks nodded his head and smiled. "Yes ma'am."

Emily found herself smiling back at him and she didn't know why. She did know there was chemistry between them and that the room had suddenly become very small.

# Chapter Twenty-Three

ROBBY BROOKS AND EMILY WORKED side by side, almost instinctively reading each other's minds as they placed the furniture.

"I can't believe you set that there," Emily said, amazed as Robby placed the oversized cherry wardrobe exactly where Emily had decided it would go months ago, when she had first seen it in the store.

"The cherry picks up the afternoon light. It fills the corner, yet doesn't overpower it. The piece belongs here."

"I know," was all she could whisper. "It looks beautiful there. For half a second I had thought it was going to be too large, but it's just perfect."

"Always go with your first instinct."

When they were finished, Emily realized she'd had fun. The thought took her aback. Arranging the furniture, giving direction, and laughing with the men had been a pleasant experience.

She felt good.

Robby glanced up at her as he gently wiped his hands with a soft cloth. "You know, you have real taste and class. You know how to decorate a room. Have you ever thought about doing it professionally?"

Emily was stunned. "No, I just enjoy putting things together."

Robby fished in his blue jeans and took out a business card. "Well, if you ever do, I could use someone with your style and eye."

Emily studied the card. "You're the owner of Berger-Yaliff Furniture? I thought you were...what are you doing delivering furniture?"

Robby looked at her and laughed. Emily liked his laugh and his smile. He was a handsome man. She laughed with him.

"Well, how was I to know?" she teased.

"I started delivering furniture twenty years ago. Sure, I own the place now. But if you don't get out sometimes, you go nuts. Just like today. This was fun. I'm serious about the job offer."

He looked around her house. "I'm sure you don't need the job, but, then again, you just might need it and not know it."

He tipped his head toward her and turned to go. His words rang through Emily's head and reached her heart. Maybe she did need something. Maybe proving her talent in decorating was just what she needed. Maybe she needed that more than drinking at ten in the morning and more than waiting on Marcus to come home and have dinner with her. She was all alone and she was tired of feeling sorry for herself. Before she could think about it, Emily heard herself speaking.

"Mr. Brooks, I would be interested in working for you. Maybe part-time. Would that be okay?"

Robby Brooks heard her say the words and had been counting to see how long it would take her to make up her mind. He stopped and turned to face her squarely. "That would be fine, Mrs. Shane. When would you like to start?"


FOR THE FIRST TIME IN A LONG time Emily felt alive. She changed her clothes three times before Marcus came home. She had fresh flowers delivered for the entire house. The house, her house, no, her home, she corrected herself, was completely finished, and tonight she was going to tell Marcus about her job.

She had already met with Robby on two occasions and made suggestions for a few of his clients. He had been thrilled with her ideas and thought she would become a top decorator in no time. He had kept his promise to not tell the clients who was making the choices, but it was getting more difficult to hide, since more and more clients were requesting "the person" who did so and so's house.

With her clout and prestige, she was sure to take decorating to new limits, he had told her. She was still giddy from her meeting with him that afternoon. Marcus had been so busy he had not had time for her. She didn't care. And more importantly, Emily realized she had not had a drink in two weeks. Her work on the house had consumed her.

She awoke early and worked on the small details herself, and then hit the stores, shopping for the perfect small antique table that must have red marble and a light oak finish to go in the corner of the study. She scoured the streets for hours looking for a ten inch high blue Crystal vase to sit on the table that would capture the sunlight every day at two. Emily had a desire to succeed. She had set goals for herself and she was reaching all of them.

Now, if only Marcus would share them with her and realize her accomplishments. Surely tonight would be the night. Emily had the servants prepare rack of lamb with a mint sauce and garlic mashed potatoes along with a chilled bottle of Dom Perignon.

She finally selected a pale periwinkle sheath that slipped over her slender body like a second skin. Sweeping her hair up into a chignon, she fastened it with a pearl and diamond clip. Looking into the mirror, she studied her reflection and liked what she saw. She had told all of the servants they were dismissed at eight o'clock sharp, so that she could spend the evening alone with Marcus. She felt the butterflies in her stomach begin to swirl.

"Finally, my masterpiece is finished!" Emily laughed out loud. And to think, she had hated this house. Not even the big bad Mrs. Shane could keep her down, try as she might. She had known Emily would hate the big house, with its overbearing walls and large rooms.

But Emily had tackled every problem the house had presented with aplomb. She had brought warmth, sophistication, and character to each room. Emily had decided the secret to decorating was to take each room and make it into a home, not a house, but someplace to truly live in and be comfortable living in.

She had a unique gift of creating a special place in each room. When someone entered any of the rooms, they felt as if they could stay and chat for a while there.

Emily heard voices downstairs and rose from the vanity table. As she walked to the door, she stopped and froze in her tracks. Marcus was home. He had brought company.

"Emily! Emily! Are you up there? Come see the surprise I brought home for you."

Emily slowly descended the winding staircase and never broke eye contact with Mrs. Abigail Shane.

"Oh, Emily dear, you look lovely. The house is absolutely stunning. When Marcus said you were going to have the big unveiling for him tonight, well, I couldn't miss the opportunity to share this occasion with you both. I do thank you for allowing me to be your guest."

Emily held back tears that were threatening to escape. Once again, her bubble had been burst.

"Oh, Mother, don't be so dramatic. You are not a guest in our home. You are family. We are delighted that your schedule allowed you to join us tonight. It makes it that much more special, doesn't it, darling?"

Emily smiled and nodded. "But of course. But of course." Emily knew not to say anything else. She held her head high.


THE HOUSE DID LOOK PICTURE perfect. Abigail Shane would have to admit that Emily had indeed transformed a cold bare house. She had made it her home.

Mrs. Shane walked from room to room inspecting the house as if she were a drill sergeant. Emily half expected her to produce a white glove and check for dust, but that was, of course, the maid's duty, not hers.

Waiting for approval proved difficult for Emily. She had envisioned Marcus going from room to room exclaiming wild excitement. Stoically, he followed behind his mother, waiting for her response.

"I must say, you have done a splendid job, Emily. Not exactly my tastes, which tend to go with the more elaborate and true 15th century antiques, but, I do like what you have done. Don't you, Marcus?"

Marcus shook his head and turned to face Emily. He put his arm around her. "You did a nice job, Emily."

Emily wanted to scream. She wanted to run from the room and tear her clothes off and leave them both standing there. She wanted to break something. She wanted to hit someone. But instead, she heard her own calm voice saying, "Thank you, Marcus. I'm glad you like it. Are we all ready for dinner? I let the help go, but everything is ready."

Why had she thought Marcus would respond any differently than he had? He had practically ignored everything around him for months on end. She would place a piece of furniture and he would walk around it. She would lay down a new throw rug and he would simply step over it, never even mentioning that he noticed it. Solomon would work in the house until dark and he had never spoken to the man.

He was so preoccupied with the future his mother had planned for him; Emily was a minor but essential step in his life. Emily knew she completed the perfect picture.

She remained quiet during dinner. She had lost her appetite, so she let the higher ranking Mrs. Shane enjoy her lamb. Emily nibbled on salad and bread while watching mother and son talk animatedly about business, current affairs, and his run for office. According to them Emily wasn't even in the room. Yes, his mother had picked out the perfect wife. She could decorate. She could entertain. She could disappear when needed.

# Chapter Twenty-Four

MARCUS CLIMBED INTO THE large bed and moved in close to Emily. He stroked her hair as she laid still. His breathing became heavier as he slid his hand gently around her neck, tracing the outline of the slender curves. Slowly and teasingly he let his fingers trace her breast. His other hand slowly and gently lifted her silk pale blue nightgown. His hands were warm on her skin. She closed her eyes and imagined that she was happy and that Marcus really loved her. Perhaps he did. Right now she felt as if he did.

She whispered, "Marcus, love me, please love me." He stifled her request with a tender kiss, which became harder as he pressed his lips then thrust his tongue into her mouth. The sensation of wanting love absorbed Emily as she almost cried out in the agony of wanting love so badly. She wrapped her arms around her husband and, for the first time in one month, they made pure and uninterrupted love. Emily was a woman fulfilled, if only for one night.

EMILY'S STEP WAS LIGHTER AND FULL of more energy as she greeted Marcus at the breakfast table. He was already dressed for work and finishing his last cup of coffee. She kissed him tenderly on the forehead and he smiled at her.

"You look like a schoolgirl this morning after a naughty night," he teased.

Emily smiled and laughed. "You should know, my sweet." She giggled.

"Campaign starts strong in three weeks, Emily. I am going to have a woman by the name of Sara get in touch with you. She will be your personal secretary during the campaign. You will have luncheons, handshaking, dinners, and a lot of functions to attend in the next four months. If I am going to win this congressional seat, it's going to take some work."

For a brief moment, Emily thought of last night. Had he made love to her to appease her? She shrugged off the idea. He genuinely seemed pleased with her. He wanted her to help. What more could a wife want?

"Sure, darling. That would be great. I have wanted to tell you that I have been helping..." Before she could finish her sentence the ringing of the telephone silenced her.

Marcus held up his hand. "Hold that thought. I've been expecting a very important call."

Marcus strode to the telephone and answered it. As he spoke to the caller, she could hear some of the conversation.

"Yes. Wonderful. That's the kind of news I like to hear...Yes, I know I did...Oh really? No, she didn't mention you...I certainly will."

Marcus hung up the telephone and came to Emily. He put his arms around her and looked deep into her eyes. They were filled with love.

"So, you've been campaigning for me on your own. That was Robert Brooks. His family owns everything from clothing stores to furniture stores. His old man is worth several billion. Anyhow, we have been hammering him hard to throw some of that cash our way. He says he met you. He said that you are a 'jewel,' and that he and his wife would be delighted to not only contribute to the campaign, but they will assist us in our efforts as well. So you don't have any other big contributors out there you've been oiling for me, do you?"

Emily could feel her face flush. Robby a billionaire? Robby married? He had never mentioned a wife, not that she cared that he was married. She had just liked his company and liked going to his store and helping him with new clients. She was going to tell Marcus about the job, but the timing had never been right. Now, here was Robby, or Robert, calling her house. Why hadn't he mentioned the job to Marcus, she wondered. Well, she would find out, because she was meeting him in less than two hours.

"No more. Sorry, dear. I met him when I bought all this furniture from him. I think he is really just giving us back some of the money we gave him!"

Marcus was amused by his wife. "Whatever you're doing, keep it up. The Brooks name being associated with ours is very good. Very good indeed."

Marcus kissed the top of her head.

"I'll have Sara call you after one o'clock today. Make sure you are available to talk. I'll be home late."

Marcus walked out of the room and left the house. Under her breath, Emily whispered a child-like, "Yes Sir."


WHEN EMILY ENTERED THE furniture store, Robby greeted her with open arms. He gave her a warm hug and ushered her back into his office.

"Good morning," he said. "So, are you ready to start on a long list of clients?"

Emily stared back at him in dismay. "Why didn't you tell me you had been talking to my husband about the campaign? Why didn't you tell me you were married? Do you have children? Do I sound weird?"

Emily burst out laughing and Robby followed suit.

After they settled down a few seconds later, Robby grew quiet.

"I figured the campaign wasn't your favorite subject," he said. "I think you need a friend, and I believe I have become your friend. If I can help you by helping him, then I want to do that. I haven't discussed my wife because we are, well, not the happiest two people in the world. She's off to do some more shopping in Paris or New York or Dallas. I am not quite sure. I have two small children for whom I care deeply and for whom I am trying my best to give the world, but right now I have to do that with the help of nannies. Not my idea of raising children.

"I leave here every day at six sharp and spend the rest of the evening with them. I don't come in until nine in the morning so that I am able to have breakfast with them. I didn't share this with you because I think you have a lot you are bearing yourself right now. I want my marriage to work and I think you do, too."

Emily looked at her folded hands in her lap. Slowly, she raised her eyes to meet his and she saw a man who had just gone to the very core of his inner self and told her his true feelings. Emily had never known a man quite like Robby Brooks. She was glad he was her friend.

"Maybe I could meet your wife and your children. Maybe we could all become friends."

Robby nodded and smiled. "I'd like that. Now, tell me why you haven't told Marcus about your job. And don't lie to me. I know you haven't told him."

Emily was exhausted when she finished telling her whole life story. She spared not one single detail. She had cried and laughed and left nothing unturned or untold. She felt liberated. Someone knew. Then it hit her. Yes, someone knew, someone who had great power and could destroy her. Before she could complete the thought, Robby rose from his desk and took her hands.

"No, Emily, your secrets are safe with me. Now and forever."

Emily believed him.

# Chapter Twenty-Five

DARCEY BROOKS WASN'T EXACTLY beautiful, but she was striking. Her jet black hair glistened when the sun hit it, and she had extraordinary cat green eyes that reminded Emily of some ancient Egyptian queen. Her eyes and her hair framed her flawless olive completion. Yet, she wasn't beautiful. Her petite build was enhanced by her slender frame and polished accents.

Everything was perfect with the woman. She had a warm smile that showed white, even teeth. Emily couldn't help but stare at her. She was really a lovely creature to look at, and she had no trouble seeing the pretty debutante and Robby together. She imagined their children must be beautiful.

Darcey was kind and friendly. The way Robby had described her struck Emily as strange, because the woman standing before her appeared to be just the opposite of that description.

In fact, Emily thought she really liked this woman.

"So, you want to go shopping today? I have a two hour time frame that we could use to hit a few stores. I have the limo and we could save a lot of time, so what do you think?" Darcey asked the question so simply she might as well have been asking whether she wanted a soda or iced tea.

"A limo to go shopping? Are you kidding?"

Darcey threw her head back and laughed. "No, I'm not kidding. I learned a long time ago, honey, that if you've got money, spend it. You can't take it with you. Besides, it saves time, energy, and it's fun!"

Emily had to laugh at Darcey's mischievous behavior and attitude.

She also had to admit she was intrigued. A limousine to go shopping? Now that was certainly decadent, but she still heard herself clearly say, "Sure. I'll go!"

DARCEY DROPPED EMILY OFF at her front porch. "If I didn't have to get a manicure and pedicure, we could have done some serious shopping. Lunch next week sound good to you?"

Emily was in high spirits. She had actually had one of the most fun days she could ever remember. "Wouldn't miss it! But, I'll drive."

Both women laughed and Emily watched the sleek black limousine snake down her driveway and then out of sight. When she came into her house she dropped her packages on the hall bench. Maybe she had so much fun because she had been with another woman. A girlfriend.

Marcus stepped out of the study and Emily gasped for breath, "My God, Marcus, you scared me. Why are you home? Is anything wrong?"

Marcus studied her closely. "No, nothing is wrong, other than my wife traipsing all over town being very showy and Miss Uppity in a limousine. Have you lost your mind?"

Emily couldn't find the words to explain. "I...I...I went shopping with Darcey Brooks and I..."

Before she could explain, Marcus cut her off. "Just how do you think it looks for a soon to be congressman's wife riding around town shopping in a limousine? Huh? Did you think of that today? Granted, you were in good company, and I do encourage you to develop a friendship with Mrs. Brooks, but use your head, Emily. You cannot let the public see you engaging in such extravagance."

Emily shook her head. She was trying to take in what he was saying. "My goodness, Marcus. It was one time, and it was fun, and it was for three hours."

He snorted. "Yes, exactly three hours. Two of which you were suppose to be home, taking calls from your personal secretary who called my office looking for you. You may continue to see Darcey Brooks, but please be wise about it. Do you understand?"

Emily nodded quietly.

"By the way, I spoke with Robert Brooks today. He and his wife will be dining here on Friday." Marcus turned and strode from the room. Emily heard the front door shut just as the telephone rang.

"Miss Sara Newcomb on the telephone for you, Madame." Emily took the phone and sat down to make her appointments for the coming campaign week.

EMILY DIDN'T FEEL WELL. SHE didn't feel like eating, and she was dizzy. She had not been resting well and she was looking forward to her day ending. Fortunately this was the final stop on her scheduled tour for the day.

The week had been grueling, with six luncheons, three dinner parties, and four speeches to various women's groups. She often wondered who else was working the campaign trail. She managed to stop by Robby's shop twice and oversee the selection of furniture for some of his projects. He always seemed genuinely pleased to see her, and that was the only time she felt like herself.

Everything Emily did was low key now. She made sure that she did nothing out of the ordinary. She had talked to Darcey three times and had a quick drink with her after a campaign lunch. Darcey would have liked to have stayed and talked, she claimed, but one of her nails had broken and she had to have it fixed before it drove her crazy.

"I have never in my life known anyone as paranoid about their nails," Emily mused.

Darcey just laughed at the comment. "Yes, well, I know it takes you two hours to get ready to go anywhere, and you yourself told me you would never let your husband see you, day or night, less than perfect. So what's a nail fetish compared to that?"

Emily smiled. "Touché. See you tomorrow at the house."

Emily looked at her watch. If she hurried, she had time to make a quick stop at Robby's store and finish her selection for the apartment building entrance for him. She knew it was on his list of things to be completed before the end of the week.

As she swung the car into the lot, she saw Robby in his car, pulling out. She beeped her horn and he greeted her.

"Hey there. Sorry, can't meet with you right now. Sam here isn't feeling too well and I've got to take him home."

Emily looked puzzled. "Why don't you call Darcey? I think she's at her manicurist."

Robby shook his head. "No, already tried. She was going there early this morning anyhow. That's why I ended up with little Sam the man here. Not that I mind. I don't know where she is."

Emily started to say something and then closed her mouth. Their affairs were none of her business. "Okay, I'll go on inside and write down my suggestions. Will that help?"

"You are the best. Still haven't told Marcus about us, though, have you?"

Emily shook her head. "As long as I can juggle everything, then right now is not a good time." Emily smiled and Robby understood.

She watched him drive off with his young son sitting next to him and wondered what Darcey was really up to. As she got out of the car, Emily had to steady herself. She knew she was going to be sick. She slowly crouched beside her car and vomited up her wonderful chicken lunch.


"CONGRATULATIONS, MRS. SHANE. YOU'RE pregnant. I'd guess about two months," Dr. Tyler Richards was saying to her. Emily was speechless. Her mind was dizzy with thought. Pregnant? Me? Marcus will kill me, she thought.

"Thank you, Doctor." Emily couldn't hear the rest of Dr. Richards's comments. She vaguely heard campaign, take it easy, and how happy he was for them. She found herself nodding and smiling and shaking his hand before getting dressed.

As Emily walked to her car, her falling tears stung her eyes. She had wanted a child for a long time, but knew it had not been the right time. When the right time was, she didn't know.

She and Marcus had never really discussed children. They had only been married just over a year. His campaign was in the final stages and he had a solid lead. She had worked very hard for him for six straight months, and put in fifty- and sixty-hour weeks for him during the last two months.

She knew the night of their lovemaking. The night the house was completely finished. That is when it happened. Marcus had really loved her that night. She had felt it. She put her hand on her stomach. Maybe this was the right time after all. She found herself smiling. Yes, maybe this was exactly the right time.

Emily was giddy with excitement. She studied her reflection in the rearview mirror and wondered what kind of mother she would be. She hesitated before starting the car. Leaning back in the seat, she thought of her own childhood, something she had tried to wipe away and forget for so long.

She stared back at herself. A determination grew within her just as her child grew. Overcome with a protective feeling she had never known, Emily gently touched her stomach. A feeling so powerful washed over her. It was as if she had always had it, but had never known it existed. Emily suddenly knew she would protect this baby with all of her might. Never would she let this child become a victim to the evils of the world. Her own mother had not been able to protect her and Emily vowed she would not let anything like that happen to her unborn child.

Keeping her hand on her stomach, Emily promised her unborn child she would never forsake her. She began to sob uncontrollably and without real reason. She let her loneliness and her hatred for all of those who had violated her sweep through her body. She cried for the twelve year old girl who had sank to her knees in the shower, bleeding and all alone so many nights ago. She cried for the young woman who had lost everything she owned to a mean spirited, deceitful man who had taken her love and part of her life. Taking a long deep breath, she studied herself in the mirror. She let the tears flow for the woman who had married wealth in search of true love because that woman so far had only found indifference while being ignored.

Emotions of torment and anguish flooded her body and engulfed her. She wasn't sure how long she had sat in her car, but a light drizzle had started to fall. She wiped her tears and started the car. She was having a dinner party tonight and she wanted the world to know about her pregnancy. She let the engine warm and she slowly pulled out into traffic. Emily turned the radio on just as a love song was beginning. For some unknown reason Emily thought of Robby, not the father of her child.


DR. RICHARDS WATCHED AS EMILY pulled away from the hospital. He picked up the telephone and leafed through Emily's file folder.

"Congratulations," he said into the receiver. "You are going to be a grandmother."

The elder Mrs. Shane politely thanked the good doctor before shutting the doors of her study. Emily was pregnant. She strummed her fingers on her desk before a smile tugged at the corners of her lips.

"Yes. A pregnancy right now just might be an asset to the campaign if I play it right," Abigail whispered quietly.

She rose from her desk and grabbed her thick rolodex. She knew she had a lot of news to get out very quickly if the announcement was going to be made by press time. A grandmother, she thought. She looked at her own reflection in the mirror. A child. It had to be a boy to carry on the name. And it would have to be named Marcus Shane III. Yes, she had a lot of work to do. She picked up the telephone as she continued to tap her fingers impatiently.

"Hello, dear. I hope I haven't caught you at a bad time. I just received the most wonderful news."

# Chapter Twenty-Six

EMILY MOVED SMOOTHLY THROUGH TRAFFIC, wondering how she would break the news to Marcus. She felt satisfied and happy, a feeling that had eluded her for some time. She discovered that her hand still rested gently on her belly.

"I wonder when you feel your baby move." Dozens of questions began flooding her mind. Had she taken any medication in the last six weeks? Had she drank any alcohol? How much had she drank?

"Better think of more important things like telling your father," Emily said aloud, patting her still flat stomach. Maybe she could buy dozens of blue and pink balloons and suspend them in the foyer so that when Marcus arrived home he couldn't help but at least wonder what they were for. Maybe a good bottle of champagne and baby booties tied to the bottle.

She had so much work to do. She wanted her baby and her pregnancy to be kept private.

Her entire life was being lived in a fish bowl right now, and she was swimming in the center of it. This would be one event she would control.

She would tell Marcus tonight, when they were alone and very private, and she would make him understand her need of keeping it quiet. She also wanted to make sure everything went well in the first twelve weeks. She couldn't bear losing her child and have the entire district knowing about it, too.

Emily deftly swung the sleek automobile into the long and winding driveway. Today is the first day of the rest of my life, Emily mused. She looked at her stomach and began talking to her unborn child. "You, little one, are, and always will be, the answer to my prayers. I know you will bring joy and happiness to me and to your father."

Emily grabbed her belongings from the car and, with a euphoric feeling, and a lighter step than she had begun her day with, she bounded into the house. There she stopped. The color drained from her face and she felt the bile rise to her throat. Her mother-in-law stood holding a dozen yellow roses. Marcus was there smiling, and a newspaper photographer stood, camera in hand, waiting to take the happy family portrait. Emily barely heard Mrs. Shane say, "Good news travels fast, my dear. We don't want to miss a good press opportunity, now do we?"

Emily ran up the stairs and threw up. Afterward, she steadied herself and clung to the rich mahogany banister, before slowly beginning her descent. Her mouth was dry and her eyes damp. She could hear the whispers and soft, hushed tones coming from the library. Marcus and his mother were discussing her child's future. Her future. Why did she think she could control anything? Her life didn't belong to her anymore. When had she given it up? The sounds of the conversation wafted up to her.

"Boy or girl, we don't care," Mrs. Shane was saying. "Just to have little feet padding through this big house will be marvelous."

"Yes, we are thrilled. My wife is in excellent condition and is already busy making nursery arrangements. Of course, she will continue to work on the campaign. In fact, it is the first thing she insisted upon!"

The press all chuckled and marveled at how gracious and wonderful Emily must be, and how proud Marcus and his mother obviously were at the news of the impending birth.

Emily cleared her throat and Marcus rose and greeted her warmly.

"I guess you are having a little morning sickness in the afternoon. Well, let's let these wonderful ladies and gentlemen have their photos so they can get on with their day. Plus, we do still have a dinner engagement here tonight."

The elder Mrs. Shane interrupted. "Yes. And since it is such a joyous occasion, Marcus and I made some calls and invited a few more guests. I hope you don't mind, dear."

The remark was laced in sweetness, but dripped with venom that only Emily could decipher. Only she could see the meanness that crept through that smile. Sighing deeply, she casually tossed her beautiful mane of golden hair behind her shoulders and smiled coyly, not to be outdone.

"Oh, that sounds lovely. Thank you for thinking ahead for me. This is really all quite nice."

Emily gracefully eased into the rich satin sofa as Marcus stepped to her side, looking surprised before asking, "Dear, you don't want the grandmother standing too, do you?"

Emily uncrossed her long legs and slid down the seat. Mrs. Shane sat coolly next to her and smiled sweetly into Marcus's eyes. Emily wondered why she was the only one in the room who could see through them. Before Emily could even think, she had already resumed her automatic pilot position following Mrs. Shane's every direction with swift and precise movements.

"Now, you need to get these two lovebirds and parents to be all alone. They don't need a doting grandmother in every picture," Abigail suggested.

The press laughed appreciatively and continued snapping away. Even the old woman had known she couldn't be in every picture. Emily smiled brightly. Of course, no one knew the questions she was asking. "When did Mrs. Shane give you permission to get pregnant?" "Was Mrs. Shane there on the night in question?" Emily was so amused with herself that she didn't hear Marcus until he cleared his throat. "That should do it, Emily."

Emily rose and escorted the large group to the front door. Her shoulders felt heavy and she cast her eyes to the floor as she walked back into the library and sank into the overstuffed wingback chair.

The three of them sat alone in the library. The room was eerily quiet, except for the soft swishing sound coming from the age old grandfather clock. Each sweep of the pendulum screamed out to Emily. She kept her hands folded in her lap as she tried to swallow.

"How did you find out so quickly?" Emily managed to finally ask.

"Oh, my dear, you should know that we Shanes find out everything. No secret is a secret long with us. By the way, I've been meaning to ask, how is your friend Robert, or is it Robby?" The older woman asked, with a pointblank stare.

Emily looked confused, but stammered, "Robby is fine. He and his wife, Darcey, will be joining us tonight, in fact."

Marcus spoke up. "No, in fact I called and cancelled them. Mother thought we only needed our very closest friends here tonight on this occasion. I sent your apologies. I told them you were under the weather and they would find out why tomorrow. Darcey was most understanding."

All Emily could do was nod her head and agree, as she softly said, "I see. Thank you for being so kind. I'm going to rest before our guests arrive."

Emily trudged up the stairs. How could it happen? Two hours ago she had been elated. She was living a dream. She had been a new wife about to fill the foyer with blue and pink balloons and pop champagne corks. Now, her heart was heavy and she felt defeated. They had beaten her again. And she didn't even have her friend, Robby, to share her news with. She hoped he understood. But for some reason, she knew they would even take that friendship away from her.

She lay down on the soft comforter and closed her eyes. Slowly, she began to drift off to sleep, and she dreamt of her unborn child and dozens of people surrounding her with love. There were so many people around her, but she couldn't find Marcus among them, only Robby in the distance.

# Chapter Twenty-Seven

ROBBY STARED AT EMILY'S picture. His heart ached for her, for he could see the pain emanating from her soulful eyes. The caption read "Congressional Candidate Marcus Shane and Wife Emily Announce Arrival of Newest Voter."

The newspaper dropped from his hand and rested with a rustle on his desk. Scanning the article, he shook his head as he read how elated the couple was with the news. The matriarch explained at length how the parents-to-be had called to deliver the good news. He would have laughed out loud had he not felt such anguish for Emily, for he knew that the article was filled with half truths and lies. It was filled with whatever the elder Mrs. Shane and Marcus had told the press to fill it with.

Robby picked up the phone, and then quietly placed the receiver in its cradle.

"No, Emily, you call me. I am here if you need me."

Surely she knew that, Robby thought. Why she hadn't wanted him there last night for the news, he didn't know or understand. Maybe she really did just want truly close friends as Marcus had explained so kindly the previous night.


THE NEXT FOUR WEEKS WERE an agonizing hell for Emily. Morning sickness set in with a vengeance and her demanding election campaign schedule was unrelenting.

"Hurry and get out of the bathroom. Clean yourself up for God's sake. You have exactly ten minutes before Sara picks you up for your daily appointments. Come on, Emily, you're not the first woman to be pregnant," Marcus seethed through the closed bathroom door.

The bathroom ceiling provided endless moments of entertainment. The swirling pattern went from curved to straight to wide strokes, creating a beautiful design. The cool rag felt good against her skin, as did the cold marble she rested on. Marcus continued his tirade outside the door.

It wasn't supposed to be like this. She started to imagine all of the what ifs in her life and decided to stop that game before she even got started. She knew long ago the what if game didn't change a thing. She was just over two months pregnant, sick as a dog, and she still had to pump the hands of factory workers or teachers and kiss someone else's child twenty four hours a day.

She had tried reaching Robby and Darcey half a dozen times since the impending birth announcement, but to no avail. An unexplainable feeling had begun to grow in the pit of her stomach each time she had been unable to reach her friends. Why hadn't they returned her calls? More importantly, why hadn't he returned her calls? The only communication with the pair had been a brief and almost terse message from Darcey that had been personally delivered by Marcus to her.

"Taking the children to Europe. Will contact you upon our return. D."

Why was she taking the kids to Europe? And where in Europe? And why was Robby joining them? Maybe that is what she really wanted to know.

Resting her elbows on the floor, the room continued to spin. Marcus's voice was taking on an edge that Emily knew all too well lately.

"Emily, the clock is ticking down. I cannot start babysitting you like a child. Come out of there, now!"

His voice was raised in anger. Emily lifted herself with all the strength she could muster and pushed her hair back into place. She eased the bathroom door open and found Marcus glaring at her.

"Do you have any idea how important this election is? We are four days away. I can't have you hugging a toilet seat. You have to get yourself together and hit the road, as they say. Now, do it." He turned on his heels and strode away without saying goodbye.


THE CROWDED BALLROOM SMELT of fried chicken. The past four days had been a blur. The hands touching her, the cafeteria style foods she threw up on a regular basis, the people, all smiling and wishing her well, but too close in her face. Weakened and tired, Emily began to worry about her health, although no one else seemed to be.

At least it was finally election night. The results were quickly coming in. The reception at the Sheraton hotel was packed with supporters. Marcus held a commanding lead and they knew his opponent would soon be delivering a concession speech, but strict orders had been given. No popping of champagne corks until a concession speech was made and accepted graciously.

Within minutes, hoots and hollers were heard ringing through the chamber as a young supporter rushed through the doors.

"He has conceded. It's official, Congressman Shane!"

Cheers erupted, and Emily's thoughts were drowned out. She watched in bewilderment as dozens of supporters crushed around her husband, each so proud of the man they had worked so hard to elect to represent them.

The first person Marcus put his arm around, thanked, and hugged was his mother. He never reached out to Emily until a photographer asked for a photo of the family.


IF EMILY HAD THOUGHT THE CAMPAIGN was busy, the days following the victory were worse. Her sickness was beginning to subside, but she remained exhausted. Her doctor stressed for her to rest, but Emily wondered when she was supposed to fit that into her schedule. She decided it was time to find out where Robby had been hiding, so she stopped by his store.

Jill, his receptionist, greeted her enthusiastically. Emily had always liked the young woman. Her auburn hair barely touched the top of her shoulders and her bangs hid a forehead that was too high. Her smile was bright and even, and the corners of her mouth turned upwards, easily showing years of being openly friendly and outgoing. Emily knew that Jill was genuinely glad to see her.

"Hello, Mrs. Shane. Congratulations on your upcoming arrival and on the election. Wow, a congressman's wife. How does it feel?"

Emily was honest. "It's overwhelming, to say the least, Jill. Is Mr. Brooks around today?"

The young woman returned Emily's confused stare. She hesitated for only a brief second.

"Mr. Brooks? Why, no. He moved to Oxnard to cover the store down there four or five weeks ago. I would have thought you would have known. His father was having a real problem down there..."

Emily didn't hear the rest of what the young girl was babbling. She walked out of the store in a trance and got into her car. Why didn't he call me? If we are friends then why wouldn't he tell me he was leaving?


ROBBY HAD A FEW QUESTIONS OF his own. He was still puzzled over Emily. Papers surrounded him, and his office was cluttered. He had worked for four weeks nonstop trying to get the store up and running in the right direction.

Darcey had taken the children and flown to Paris and asked for a divorce. Emily had refused his telephone calls, obviously siding with Darcey, as Marcus had told him. He had nothing left to do but to sink his teeth into his work, forget about his marital problems, and forget about the woman he thought he knew and could trust. How wrong he had been about Emily. Marcus told him how she had convinced Darcey that he was wrong for her and was just using her. It didn't sound like the Emily he knew. But did he really know her that well?

The biggest surprise had been Emily's ruse. Here he had thought the decorating job had been kept a secret from Marcus. He had actually believed her when she told him she needed the time to express herself.

Boy, what a sucker he had been. Robby shook his head in embarrassment when he recalled Marcus saying he knew all along about Emily's job. He regaled how she intimately discussed her projects in detail with him. He certainly knew every single job she had worked on, what she had ordered from him, and even the selections she had made.

Why would Emily lie to him? Why had he trusted her? And why, as it had turned out, had Marcus been the good guy after all? Robby shook his head. He didn't have the answers. He knew that Marcus was a hard working man who would be good for the district. He was glad that he had won the election. He believed the man was serious about the job, not just a politician. Too bad he had a conniving wife. Darcey had made a fool of him and so had Emily. Robby was through with women. He was even through with women that he thought had been just his friend.

# Chapter Twenty-Eight

EMILY SAT ON THE EDGE OF THE cold steel table watching the young nurse arrange a variety of instruments on a small side table. She guessed her to be about twenty five. She was pretty, but had a hard edge to her face. Her jaw was set and her lips, while full and slightly upturned, showed no warmth or sensuality. They were as set as her jaw. Emily wondered if the girl ever smiled or laughed. Her eyes were a lovely shade of blue-green, but they reflected only efficiency. No merriment or spirit danced in them.

"Here. Disrobe completely and put this on," she directed, almost tossing the starched white gown in her lap.

"Dr. Richards will see you in a few minutes. He probably won't be pleased that you've gained six pounds since your last visit," she said, never showing any emotion one way or the other toward Emily.

"I know. I seem to be huge. I can't get enough to eat. I am always starving."

The nurse just shrugged. "Your body. Harder to get it off than put it on. Now, put this sheet around you and put your clothes in the closet."

The door closed with a quiet thump and Emily was alone with her thoughts. Her hands slid over her full round belly for the tenth time in five minutes. Her belly button protruded slightly. She'd felt the baby kick more than once. Her stomach was getting big and she was hungry all the time. Everyone seemed to want to tell Emily when and what to eat.

Abigail Shane had been downright rude to her when she regaled her with the story of how she had only gained twelve pounds during her entire pregnancy with Marcus. Her voice was laced with sarcasm as she explained how she had bounced right back to her normal pre-pregnancy, slender weight before leaving the hospital.

Dr. Richards interrupted her walk down memory lane, which was fine with Emily, because any memory of Marcus's mother was not pleasant.  His white hair was bushy and unkempt. His thick black-rimmed glasses covered most of his face, giving him the look of a mad scientist.  But, Marcus's mother had insisted and, thereby, Marcus had insisted that Dr. Richards was to be her physician. She studied the aging man. His frame was still large and strong, although a slight slump and roundness was forming in his shoulders and becoming noticeable.

Emily could tell he had been a very handsome man at one time in his life. She wondered what color his full head of white hair had been. A dashing tall man with wavy blond locks, or shiny jet black hair perhaps. She couldn't tell and she didn't feel like asking.

"Let's have a listen. You've gained too much weight. Next visit, I don't want more than two pounds on you, young lady. Not good for you and not good for the baby."

His stethoscope touched her belly and she flinched. It took a few seconds for her skin to adjust to the cold instrument. Dr. Richards moved it back and forth on her belly. Emily immediately noticed the intensity in his eyes and the small furrows that deepened on his brow. He listened closely. Emily could feel the fear rise in her throat.

Oh my God, she thought. He doesn't hear a heartbeat. My baby. Something is wrong. She wanted to ask but found that she couldn't speak. She was frozen.

Dr. Richards finally broke the silence. "Emily, you may be gaining more weight for a reason. You are pregnant with twins."

Tears immediately welled up in her eyes and rolled down her cheeks. If she had ever been happier she could not remember when that particular time had been. With a renewed sense of self-confidence, she looked at the old doctor and stated flatly and directly so as to not be misunderstood.

"Dr. Richards, you are not to call Mrs. Shane with this news. I will be the one to tell my husband the news, and I will be the one to tell my mother-in-law the news. Do I make myself absolutely and perfectly clear?"

He gently chuckled and returned her direct stare. Abigail Shane just might have met her match at last in this young woman.

"I haven't the slightest idea what you are inferring. I wouldn't dream of telling anyone your news. You may get dressed."

Emily watched him turn on his heels and absentmindedly smooth his white jacket as he retreated from the room. That's one little victory, she thought to herself. Twins. Emily couldn't believe her good fortune.

"TWINS," MARCUS SHOUTED. "I can't believe you're having twins!"

Emily was surprised by his outburst. "I thought you would be thrilled, Marcus. And it's not me having twins, it's us having twins," she said.

"No, Emily I am not thrilled. As a congressman's wife, I need you right now. There are functions every single night. The pressure is enormous. I could use some help from you. My mother has to pick up the slack because you're always too tired. The only good thing about twins is that it gives me more of a chance to have a son. This is it, Emily. Twins. Shit. No more children after this. We have campaigns to run and bigger fish to fry in this political arena. Do you understand?"

Emily felt the blood go to her face. She was angry. She shouted and defended herself.

"I didn't get pregnant all by myself, Marcus. Fine. No more children. But don't expect me to be an absent mother just so you can work my butt off for some campaign. Have you got that?"

Fury flew over his face. For a moment she thought she had stepped over the line. She knew he was going to strike her. As his hand went into the air she ducked and he lashed out at emptiness. The swishing sound of his hand breezed over her head. He prepared to hit her again and she stood tall this time, waiting for the blow to come. Instead, Marcus looked at her and tears came to his eyes. "I don't know why I just did that to you, Emily. I am so sorry."

He walked out of the room, leaving her alone once again. Emily felt truly sorry for him. His mother had dominated and controlled him and never loved him. The woman he called mother had only prepared him for his role in life to satisfy whatever she wanted him to become. She had decided on politician. So, he was a politician.

Emily wondered if Marcus would have been happier being able to remain a simple but talented attorney. He had been happy then, she thought. When she had first met Marcus, he had a bounce in his step. He thrilled at the legal challenge of helping. Now, he set about to change the world. Change it however his mother decided it should be changed.


EMILY WAS DUE WITHIN five weeks. She laid on the chaise lounge, soaking in the warm spring afternoon sun. She felt good and she felt ready to give birth. Her months of pregnancy had been difficult, but Emily would not and had not complained. She wanted to be a mother. With that thought, her mind drifted to her own mother. She would like someone with her when the twins arrived. Not the nanny Abigail had arranged and not the old woman herself. The thought made Emily physically shudder.

Emily didn't have any close friends. She didn't know where Darcey was living and she hadn't heard from Robby since before she found out she was pregnant.

On impulse, and without consulting Marcus—and without knowing why she was making this decision—Emily picked up the telephone and called her mother.

Marjorie's voice was warm and soothing to Emily's ear.

"Mother? Hi, it's Emily."

Emily could hear her mother catch her breath in surprise.

"Mother, are you there?"

Emily might have cried if she had known that Marjorie's hands were trembling. Little did she know how the aging woman had waited for her only daughter to call for more than a year.

Marjorie and her husband, Wally, had followed the election closely and had even subscribed to Emily's local paper. They had been overjoyed upon seeing Emily's picture announcing the birth of their grandchild. She wondered now if Emily was calling to tell her the news of the birth.

"Yes, Emily, I'm here honey." Time vanished once again for Emily. She found it hard to swallow and fought back tears that had built up. Before she could hold back, Emily began talking, and the words started tumbling from her, almost begging her mother to come to her.

"Mom, I'm pregnant with twins and I'm due in five weeks, and I'm a little scared, and I was wondering if you would come and stay with me and help for a few weeks, and I'll pay your airfare and everything."

Emily stopped. She realized she had just said more to her mother in one minute than she had in a year. Only silence greeted her from the other end of the line. It then dawned on Emily that perhaps her mother and father were angry with her.

What she didn't know was that her mother couldn't speak because she was crying. It seemed as if the silence lasted several minutes. But, finally her mother spoke in a quiet, hushed tone.

"Yes, Emily. I will be there for you. I wouldn't miss it for the world. Your Daddy's been asking about you. He isn't getting any younger. And Emily? Your dad, he's..." She stopped and didn't continue.

"He's what, Mother?" Emily prodded.

"Oh, he's just been missing you, that's all. When do you want me there?"

The mother listened to the daughter make all the arrangements and she smiled. Her Emily was so grown up and about to become a mother herself. Of twins, no less. She hung up the telephone and faced her husband. His face was ashen and his cough was getting worse. She propped the pillows behind his head to make him more comfortable.

"That was our Emily. She wants me to come out there and stay in her fancy house and help her with her new youngins. She's gonna have twins. Twins. You're gonna be a grandpa twice over."

Wally looked into his wife's eyes. He smiled a weak smile. They both knew his time was limited as the deadly cancer cells raced through his body, destroying all his healthy cells and eating them as fast as they could. He was determined to stay alive and at least see a picture of his grandchildren. He believed that's what had kept him alive.

"I'll bring you back the best pictures in the world. And, if I can, I'll get Emily to come see you with 'em, too."

She knew Emily would never bring her children back home. She knew Emily would never return to her childhood home again. Why? She didn't know. She had her thoughts on the subject, but she never discussed them and she tried not to think about such thoughts. She knew that was the best way to handle those delicate matters. Evidently, as she thought to herself, if what she thought was true, it hadn't hurt Emily. But still, Emily would not return here.

She smiled at her ailing husband. "Yes, I'll just see if I can't talk that girl of yours into coming home." If it gave her husband something to live for, she would have told him anything.

# Chapter Twenty-Nine

*E*MILY DIDN'T FEEL WELL. She picked up her calendar and slid her fingers down the list before her. Lately it was filled with engagements for groups she had never heard of.

"Women of Wildlife," mused Emily. "What, they go out and pick flowers and they want me to entertain them at lunch? Oh, this one is priceless. 'The New Woman's Book Club.' Whatever happened to 'The Old Woman's Book Club?' " She sighed heavily as she laid the calendar down, wondering why the wife of the congressman had to go to these things. "When did I run for luncheon mate and get elected?" She picked the calendar back up and scanned the daily events.

"Yuck. Another luncheon. You two are going to turn into fried chicken and potato salad. Either that or roast beef. I promise never to make you eat any of that stuff when you grow up!"

She rested her hand on her stomach and laughed, despite her aching body. Everything hurt. Her lower back had a striking pain and her legs felt a little numb.

She slowly made her way to the telephone in the large master bedroom. She leaned against the doorframe as she scanned the room. She loved this room. It had been a labor of love when she decorated it.

Emily remembered the first time she had laid eyes on the yellow damask satin material. She had known, instinctively, that both the material and the rich burgundy satin trim she had selected were perfect for the drapes. A heavier material in mint green sprinkled around the room gave a collective cohesiveness to the surroundings. A tablecloth, a matching pillow, and a small ottoman tied everything together. The woman at the upholstery and material shop had looked skeptically upon Emily when she was making the purchases.

"Are you planning on using these pieces next to each other? I mean, these three colors and material together?"

Emily had known all along that they would be beautiful together. She never doubted her style. Her life choices maybe, but her style, never.

Emily had a flair for everything, from clothes to furniture to selecting material, and that flair had been with her all of her life and was the one thing that had not failed her. Emily smiled at the memory as she looked around the room. It did look beautiful and the magazine *Homes of Today* had thought so, too.

She wondered if the saleswoman had ever seen a copy of the article featuring her bedroom. At one time she had briefly entertained the thought of sending her a copy anonymously, but decided that would not be a polite thing to do, especially for a congressman's wife.

Emily sat down in the overstuffed chair with the heavy mint green brocade. Picking up the telephone, she groaned. Sara was not in the office, and this forced Emily to leave a message with her most disagreeable secretary.

"Just tell Sara I can't possibly make the luncheon this afternoon. I feel terrible, and the only place I am going is back to bed. Please tell her to call me when she gets this message so I will know that she has confirmed my apologies to the Ladies Garden Club. I'm sure they will understand. After all, I am three weeks from my due date with twins." Emily noticed her voice sounded hard and stressed as she spoke the last sentence.

"Well, Mrs. Shane, I am sure Miss Collins will relay your message to the necessary parties. Thank you." It wasn't that Margaret Turner disliked Emily, she just valued her job. Right now, she knew who was important, and who was merely there. She intended to play the game right because she knew Congressman Shane wouldn't be Congressman for long. His aspirations were much higher.

The buzzing sound of Sara's intercom interrupted the silence in the room. Margaret Turner relayed the message and didn't wait for a reply. She knew better. She was merely a messenger. The parties listening to the message could do with the information as they wished.

"Well, the missus doesn't sound like a happy camper, now does she, Congressman?" Sara said sarcastically, as she snuggled closer to Marcus on the makeshift bed. He was not amused.

He jumped up from the bed, grabbing a towel. He briskly walked into the bathroom and Sara could hear the shower running. Minutes later, he reemerged with his robe around him. She loved the early mornings with Marcus. She knew someone with his schedule, with the demands placed on him, needed release, and she was more than happy to oblige.

Marcus picked up the telephone and dialed, annoyed. When he spoke, it wasn't so much a conversation as a demand.

"Emily, Sara just telephoned me to say you were ill and not up to your luncheon. I have told her not to cancel your appointment. I'm sure if you rest for a few more hours you will be fine for the Garden Club. Need I remind you, three of those women's husbands were very large contributors to my campaign? I'll have someone pick you up before one. Goodbye."

Marcus didn't wait for a response and he didn't even say hello or ask how Emily felt. Sara watched him move back into the bed. She felt a twinge of guilt and thought she felt sorry for Emily, but as soon as Marcus kissed her, she forgot about his very pregnant, sick wife.

Emily placed the telephone back into its cradle. She slumped against the pillows. Why was Marcus being so inconsiderate? Why would he want to jeopardize her health or their children's health? The telephone rang again, startling Emily. Maybe it was Marcus coming to his senses. She picked it up, half expecting to hear his voice.

"Hello, Emily," cooed Abigail Shane.

"How are you and my dear boys feeling today?"

Emily braced herself for yet another confrontation. "We are fine, and like I've said before Abigail, they might just be girls."

The woman just scoffed at the idea. "My dear, there is one thing I can tell you, the Shanes have very strong genes, and they always produce boys first. I still don't know why you insisted on doing the nursery in yellow and green. Blues would have been safe, trust me. Now, I'm calling because I am having silver plate sets done for each of them, and I am putting their names on each. Marcus tells me you have decided on Marcus Shane III and Steven James, after his grandfather."

Emily didn't hear the rest of what Mrs. Shane said because she felt the room spinning. Then she heard herself crying and speaking at the same time.

"I haven't decided on any names, much less those names. No one has talked to me about names. And I am not going to talk to you now."

Emily slammed the telephone down. She felt a sharp pain seer through her body. She wished her mother were there. She felt like a little girl. All she wanted right now was someone to hold her and stroke her hair. Someone to tell her she was loved. She grabbed at her stomach. She felt weak, and when she looked down she saw the blood streaming down her leg, staining the beautiful pale yellow carpet.

# Chapter Thirty

"SHE'S BEEN THROUGH AN incredible ordeal. I really don't understand why she insisted on keeping all of those engagements, knowing full well she could be endangering her children," the deep voice scolded in the background. Emily tried to open her eyes but it was taking a considerable effort to do so.

The voice droned on and continued to berate her. "If she doesn't stay in bed, she'll kill herself." Finally a voice that Emily recognized all too well spoke.

"Oh, we will make sure she gets all of the rest she needs. I tried on more than one occasion to intervene and told her she would be harming my grandchildren. But, no. She wouldn't listen to me or to Marcus. She just absolutely insisted on going to each and every public engagement. She should have known, just as Marcus told her countless times, that the public would certainly understand. I mean, she was pregnant."

The words hurt her, but the "was pregnant" part hurt even more. What had happened to her babies?

Emily's eyes flashed open. She tried to sit up but was too weak to. "Where are my babies?"

Kind eyes peered down at her. The young doctor couldn't have been more than forty years old. His skin was dark and smooth. His jet black hair glistened against the stark bright hospital lights. Wearing a simple white lab coat over a pale blue dress shirt with a stethoscope draped loosely around his neck, his black pearl eyes studied her closely. Emily stubbornly returned his stare and thought she saw sympathy.

Her mouth was dry but she tried hard to swallow. Before she could speak, Abigail slid in beside the doctor. Both stood above her, looking down. Mrs. Shane shook her head accusingly. Finally, the doctor with the kind eyes broke the awkward silence.

"Your children are going to be fine. They are in the neonatal intensive care unit at this moment. Your husband has been with them. I really can't believe you have continued to carry such a heavy schedule Mrs. Shane."

Emily knew that any attempt to exonerate herself would fall on deaf ears. No one would believe that she had been forced to make each public appearance. She fell silent as the doctor continued.

"We took both children by cesarean section approximately two hours ago."

Emily found strength and courage she didn't know existed. A primal instinct arose in her. She wanted her children and she wanted them now.

"Take me to them."

The doctor shrugged, looking at the elder Mrs. Shane. Emily thought she detected understanding, maybe even more.

"All in good time. You just rest." He patted her hand gently, picked up his file folder, and headed toward the door.

He managed about three steps before he stopped in his tracks as Emily's voice took on a guttural sound, and she repeated, "Take me to my children, now."

Turning slowly to face Emily squarely, he nodded as a very slight smile slipped across his lips.

"Very well. I will send a nurse with a wheelchair to get you."

Emily didn't even know if she had delivered two boys or two girls. She just knew her children were alive and would be okay. She didn't wait for the wheelchair.

Through pain and determination, Emily swung her legs to the side of the bed. Her mother-in-law watched with a strange fixed stare that could have been mistaken for admiration had Emily not known her so well.

Easing herself slowly from the bed, Emily grabbed her robe and tied it neatly around herself. Slowly, and with great care and caution, she began the walk from her hospital room to the ICU where her children awaited her.

Keeping her head poised high, it took twenty minutes to reach her newborn babies. When she reached the unit she saw Marcus holding a baby wrapped in a blue blanket. Boys! Emily thought. "I had twin boys." she whispered.

Her step picked up and the pain seemed so far away now. A joy and love she had never known existed deep inside of her and enveloped her as her heart beat wildly.

Nearing the tiny creature, she could hear Marcus gently cooing to their baby boy.

"Yes, you are the best baby in all of the land. You shall inherit all that I have. You will always be my one and only."

Emily wondered why this child was being blessed so by Marcus. Then, she became all too aware of the reason. Three bassinets down lay Emily's other child, which was a beautiful, angelic little girl that Marcus wouldn't touch.

# Chapter Thirty-One

MARJORIE ANDERSON ARRIVED TWO days after the twins were born. Although Marcus was not openly rude to her, it was obvious that he didn't want her there. Neither did his mother. But neither Marjorie nor Emily really cared what either of them thought or wanted.

"Can you believe I'm a mother?" Emily gushed as Marjorie fluffed her pillow for the tenth time in one hour.

"Look at her little fingers," she said lovingly, as she stroked her daughter's tiny hands.

"I never knew I could love something or someone this much. Caroline Millicent Shane. I love her name. She'll probably hate me one day for naming her Millicent and accuse me of ruining her life because of it. But, I hope she'll understand how important it was for me to include her great grandmother in her life," Emily reasoned as she touched the locket around her neck.

"I'm sure she will grow to love her name as you do, and she will be wise enough to understand," Marjorie said simply.

Marjorie held an extra blanket in her hand and laid it gently over mother and sleeping child. She walked over and carefully lifted Steven James from his bassinet.

"Do you want to trade for a while? It's about his feeding time."

Emily had been emphatic about breastfeeding her children, much to Marcus's chagrin and his mother's outright disgust. But there had been no compromising. Emily had made up her mind and, fortunately, she had her mother's help.

Her mother's presence had made the six daily trips to the nursery so much easier, and it had allowed her to discover an inner strength she liked. She knew she was drawing it from her children. She also knew that they needed her to be strong.

SIX DAYS LATER, EMILY WAS finally released from the hospital with Caroline and Steven James. While the moment and event was one to be cherished, it was also to be shared.

Mrs. Shane had arranged for the hordes of photographers to be waiting just outside the hospital. And then there were the chosen few who were actually allowed outside of their home waiting patiently and expectantly for the new parents and children to arrive home.

Emily held Caroline tightly as Marcus proudly and defiantly showed Steven James to the dozens of well wishers. The tiny infant flinched at the bright popping flashes of the cameras and raised his red fist in the air, causing Marcus to laugh and quip, "Well, here's another Shane ready to take on the media." Emily just sighed as the photographers and journalists smiled with glee at the photo op and story.

"HERE, MARCUS, TAKE CAROLINE while I feed Steven James," Emily said.

Marcus looked at her and smiled. He walked over to Steven James and tenderly stroked his forehead. "You eat good, little man. You've got lots to do," he cooed, and breezed out of the room.

Marjorie quickly took the sleeping Caroline from her mother's arms. Emily looked up as tears threatened to spill onto her cheek.

"She's his daughter. It's as if she doesn't exist. I don't understand."

Her mother gently rocked the baby. "Don't fret. All in good time. All in good time. Isn't that right, Miss Caroline?"

But Emily didn't believe her. She knew all the time in the world wasn't enough. Marcus would never accept sweet Caroline.

"IT SEEMS LIKE YOU JUST got here. I don't think I can do all of this by myself, Mother. Do you really have to go home?"

"Well, I don't want your father to have to send a search party after me. Besides, I don't think I've ever been away from him this long. Nearly four weeks, and he didn't sound so good," her voice trailed off.

"What do you mean?" Emily asked, suddenly concerned.

"Oh, nothing. Aunt Eunice has been watching him and taking care of him. I think he's just homesick for me, that's all. Trust me. You got plenty to worry with here than to start worrying about your Daddy," Marjorie said reassuringly.

"Mother, I'm going to miss you. Thank you. Thank you for coming. Thank you for all of your help." Tears slowly trickled down Emily's face as she hugged her mother.

For some odd reason she wondered if she would ever see her again. She had no idea why she felt that way. She did know that she had rediscovered her mother's love. There truly was a special bond between a mother and a daughter. No matter what had crossed under or over the bridges of their lives, she felt all was mended and washed away. Her tears fell freely and honestly and she didn't even try to hide them or stop them.

"Thanks again. Tell Daddy he has to come out next. Promise me."

Her mother looked at her and for a brief second she entertained the thought of telling Emily her father would never return for a visit; and that if she didn't get on that plane right now with her she would never see her father alive again. But she didn't.

"Oh, Emily. You know your father. He ain't one for traveling too much."

Emily smiled. She handed her mother an envelope. "Now, don't open this until you get home. I mean it, Mother. And tell Daddy I love him, and his grandkids love him, too."

Her mother smiled through her own tears, "Oh, I'll tell him that all right. You can bet on it."

Emily's mother was true to her word. She didn't open the envelope until she got home. Inside, she found two pictures of the twins. All smiles and looking beautiful. She also found ten thousand dollars in cash, along with a note.

*"Dear Mother and Daddy,*

*This is to repay you for your love, which I have missed out on. This is to also let you have some extra income to maybe come and see me and the children when you can. Things have happened in all of our lives that I am not proud of. I am glad that I can help change some things. Others cannot be changed and, therefore, I cannot dwell on them any longer. New beginnings are here with my children. I can't wait to see you again. I love you. Emily."*

Marjorie felt older than her sixty-five years. She pressed the note close to her chest and cried openly. A pent up rage and unshed tears unleashed a fury in her as she pounded her own chest. She could read between the lines. She knew what she had long suspected was true.

"Oh, Emily, I am so sorry," she sobbed. She looked down at the envelope and reread the note.

"No, sweetheart, I just don't think that is possible."

But the money would not be used to visit her. Instead, it would be used to bury her father. Perhaps not right now, but soon. Very soon.

"I CAN'T BELIEVE THE TWINS WILL be one in just two days," Emily said with a sigh, while watching her children sleep. Steven James's mouth twitched slightly in his sleep. His chubby fingers were curled in fists, as if ready for battle. His fat, cherubic cheeks brought yet another smile to Emily's lips. Her sweet little man.

Caroline stirred in her crib. Emily walked over to find the angelic child looking up at her, anticipating her mother's every move.

"Oh, thought we'd get in a little alone time did you?"

Emily lifted the little girl and held her close to her bosom. She loved these quiet moments each morning before the household awakened and telephones rang and the busy life of her existence started. Caroline cooed softly. Emily gently brushed and stroked her eyebrows. As she did, Caroline's large blue eyes followed her mother's movements.

The jarring noise of the telephone made Emily jump, and this startled Caroline.

"I'm sorry baby. Mommy didn't mean to frighten you. It's ok."

Emily held the whimpering child close to her as she walked down the landing to retrieve the blaring instrument.

"Who on earth would be calling at six in the morning? This had better be good."

Emily snatched up the telephone and before she could even say hello, she heard her mother's cry. It was then that Emily heard her own voice, although she couldn't believe she was speaking the words.

"I'll be there as soon as I can."

# Chapter Thirty-Two

*E*MILY PACED WILDLY ACROSS the lush mint green carpet. She wound the long strand of cultured pearls that hung from her neck around her fingers, feeling the urge to yank the strand harshly and cause the silk thread to break so that the beautiful white balls would scatter across the room. She was so hurt, so frustrated, and so lonely and angry that she hardly knew how to express herself. This was the first time she could remember in a long time that she truly felt hate and despair at the same time.

"I just can't believe this is open for discussion, Emily. Your father didn't die. He's sick. Why must you play Florence Nightingale and run off across the country to attend to his needs?"

"You're really not serious, are you? Even you can't be this heartless."

"Emily, I'm sorry. It's just that it is a constant state of running. I need to get re-elected because the Senate campaign won't be a cakewalk. It will be difficult. I need you too," he said sweetly, brushing the hair away from her face.

"Marcus, my father is on his deathbed. I am not being melodramatic. I can feel it. I am leaving on that plane tonight. I will fly all night to be with him. I have made arrangements with Mrs. Carson for the children. Extra help will come each day and she will keep her regular schedule at night. Trust me, you will not have to alter any of your day to day activities," she said flatly. "It would have been nice, or should I say, comforting, to have had your support in this decision. You know how hard it is for me to return."

"How long will you be gone? I need to let Sara know when she can start bookings for you again."

"Just tell Sara I'll get back to her," Emily said sharply, as she opened her huge walk-in closet doors and flung her suitcase to the floor.

Marcus started to say something else then actually thought better of it before leaving the room.

Emily inhaled deeply and counted to ten. She could do this. Going home was one thing, but leaving her children for the first time overnight was another.

"Okay, my sleeping prince and princess. Mother loves you. Mother will return to you. Mother will always protect you."

Smiling, she kissed Steven James and smoothed his blanket around him. He tossed his head from side to side then snuggled closer to the soft material. Caroline stirred in her crib. Emily fingered her silky soft blonde curls and kissed her tenderly on her forehead.

"I love you angel."

# Chapter Thirty-Three

THE SUN WAS CRESTING OVER the mountains of East Tennessee, and the vista it provided took Emily's breath away. Looking down on the vivid display of colors provided by the changing maple, oak, and elm trees, it looked too brilliant to be real. An artist would have a hard time capturing the true beauty that lay beneath her.

Seattle was beautiful, with its fall foliage and the cold wintry nights, but this was nature bursting against a sky so blue and utterly amazing that it was almost too much to view. She closed her eyes, wanting to remember, to burn this image in her mind forever.

Emily tried to count the different hues of oranges and yellows, and the pale soft browns compared to the mahogany browns and the rich, earthy deep browns. The mingling of colors created a palette of colors only God could have created. She loved autumn. She had forgotten that autumn in Tennessee was a truly awe inspiring experience.

Stepping off the plane, a gust of crisp fresh air sent a chill up Emily's spine.

"Stay steady. You're here now," she repeated to herself.


EMILY FOUND HER FATHER'S ROOM on the fifth floor of Baptist Hospital in south Knoxville. His body looked so small and frail, outlined against the oversized hospital window overlooking the Tennessee River below.

Knoxville was beautiful at this time of year. The river snaked through the edge of the city and created a fringe or border for the southern portion of the downtown area. The changing trees transformed the business district, causing it to resemble a romantic hideaway snuggled against the backdrop of the Great Smoky Mountains. Usually, the city was a dull gray outlined with older red brick buildings and decaying concrete. A typical southern city a little past its prime. It especially looked harsh against a bleak, dreary winter sky that settled over the city for so many months each year.

But Knoxville was at its prettiest during the fall months. Except maybe in the spring, when the azaleas, hundreds of dogwoods, tulips, and daffodils took over, Emily mused. Knoxville in the springtime was lovely, too. While Emily debated the changes in seasons and the scenic possibilities that were to be seen in this East Tennessee city, her father awakened.

"Hey, Daddy, I'm here. It's me, Em."

A weak smile pressed against his lips. His eyes weren't their vivid blue but a watery, paler version. The mischief in them was gone. But the love was there. He was sick. He was dying and Emily knew it. She closed her own eyes and gently rubbed his cold, paper thin hands and held them tightly.

"Thank you dear God for letting me get here. Just to let me hold his hand and look into his precious eyes one more time."

The hospital room was eerily quiet. An occasional beep, the call for a doctor or nurse, could be heard from speakers in the hallway.

Her father's breathing echoed through the room as it became slightly more labored. Emily continued to hold his hand. She stroked his face and his eyebrows, just as she did her own children's. She wondered if he had done this to her as a child.

Marjorie arrived just before seven that night. She hugged Emily tenderly and held her for a long moment. The two shared a world of understanding as they stood before her father's bed.

"Emily?" Her father's weak voice broke their silence.

"Yes, Daddy? I am right here."

"How's that sweet Caroline and Steven James?"

"Growing so big. Just wait until you see them. Now, you rest, because you have to get better so you can come to my house for Christmas." She choked on her own words.

"Yes, that would be nice. Christmas with Emily and the children. I love you, Emily."

"I love you, too Daddy."

Emily hung her head and cried softly as her father's breath slowly but surely became slower and more difficult for him. She held his hand, trying with all of her might to keep life in his failing body. She gently let her thumb rub each finger and would turn his hand over in hers, trying to keep it warm. But her attempts were to no avail. Emily's father died shortly after midnight on her children's first birthday.


SEVIERVILLE, TENNESSEE HAD, by some people's standards, grown by leaps and bounds. It now had close to twenty hotels, a few of them major chains, but they were still small. Emily stayed in a newer hotel. She pulled the thick orange and green paisley print curtain aside as she waited and watched for her father's sister, Eunice, to pick her up for the receiving of friends at the funeral home.

This is what she had dreaded. This is the night of nights she knew would come at some point in her life. The time was now when she would have to face her uncles. It wasn't that she hadn't seen them since that terrible night so many years ago. But it was the first time she would face them as an adult who wanted to hold them accountable for destroying a little girl's dreams and life.

Of course, she had never thought it would be at the funeral home with friends and family passing through, mourning the death of one of her parents. But she knew it would come. What would she say to them? How would she react to them? Should she ignore them? Should she march up to them and kick them and spit in their faces and go through her speech, which she had rehearsed so many times in her life?

Now that the time had come, she didn't know what to do. She felt sick to her stomach. The telephone rang, causing her to jump as a small cry escaped from her lips. Upon hearing her mother's tired and exhausted voice, Emily felt stronger.

"Em, I just wanted to tell you not to worry about anything tonight. I mean, nobody is gonna be there tonight to cause you any problem," Marjorie managed to get out.

Emily could tell that her mother didn't know how or what to say. Even though her voiced was ravaged with sorrow it was also drained with defeat, loneliness, and guilt. Emily's heart ached for her mother. She wanted to simply say it was okay and that she understood, but she let her continue.

"You got enough on ya and I just never did discuss it with you and, well, I figured a lot out, Emily. I ain't seen hide nor hair of Roy or Delbert in over a year. Since I read your note. Emily, I am sorry. If your Daddy had known, he would've killed them."

Emily just held the telephone close to her ear and realized her hands were trembling.

The headlights of her aunt's car swinging into the parking space in front of her window brought Emily out of her trance.

"New beginnings, Mom. Aunt Eunice is here. I'll see you at the funeral home."

And that had been it. Emily slowly put the telephone back in its cradle and swallowed hard as a single tear made its way down her cheek. All those years of anguish, hate, and pain. The pure pent up rage of a lifetime just talked about in so few words. New beginnings, Emily thought. "Oh, Daddy, I miss you so much already."


A LIGHT FROST COATED THE GROUND and the morning light danced across the grass because of the moisture. It was colder than normal, but it was a glorious day, Emily thought. Blue skies. Crisp fresh air. Smoldering Smoky Mountains with the blue-gray mist hanging over the ridges and stillness. "This is the day my Daddy will be buried," Emily said softy.

Emily was still in shock and was physically exhausted by the past few days. Isolating herself in her hotel room, not wanting to spend too much time at her parent's house had been a wise choice. She had stayed the first day at the hospital until her Father had died, and then she went straight to the hotel. Marjorie had never once questioned her decision.

Walter Lee Anderson was to be laid to rest shortly before noon at Hillvale Memorial Park. Emily glanced out the window of the small hotel room and thought of her children. She missed them, but was thankful she had come.

It had been life changing for Emily. She knew deep in her heart that she would never have forgiven herself had she not come to him. She almost felt lucky. The cancer had slowly taken her father's life over the past three years, Emily had learned. But in the end he had won his own battle against it because he had waited on her to get there before he succumbed to it. He knew she would come to him. And come she had. Her Daddy. "Yes, he would have killed them if he had known," she whispered.

"MOTHER, I WANT YOU TO COME FOR A visit in the early spring. It'll do us both good," Emily said as she hugged her mother goodbye. She was ready to get back to her life in Seattle and to her children. It was unbelievable how much she missed Caroline and Steven James.

"I'm glad you stopped by before you left. I didn't know if you would. I would have understood. I'll get out there, I promise.

The taxi cab's motor idled loudly in the driveway. Emily put her arms around her mother one last time and squeezed hard. "I love you, Mother. Goodbye."

Emily settled into the dingy backseat, letting her head rest against the faded forest green vinyl faux leather. She studied Wayne Dickens's taxi cab driver's permit posted next to the meter lever. Wayne puffed on his Marlboro, letting the thick blue smoke curl from his nose and mouth. With every other intake he would blow smoke rings, this while he slowly pulled away from the street where Emily had grown up. He then got onto the main highway that leads through Sevierville.

She watched as the tiny town nestled in the hills rolled by. Up ahead, a small traffic jam was causing a backup on the main road. With only four lights on the road, traffic jams were a little unusual.

"Looks like we got somebody hurt up here," Wayne announced officially. He slowed the car, rolling his window down to peer out, not to help or offer assistance, but just to get a better look at the situation. Emily, too, leaned forward to study the commotion. There in the road lay a man, bleeding. His battered and bloody body lay lifeless on the cold pavement. Another man, who was shaking with stooped shoulders, and was apparently racked with sorrow, bent over him. It was in that instant that Emily recognized him.

Roy slowly turned his head around, almost as if he sensed her presence. He immediately caught Emily's eye. He returned her stare through thick bloodshot eyes. His stance was shaky and feeble. Emily realized it wasn't so much the tragedy before him making him woozy as the fact that he was drunk. She also realized that the man he hovered over was Delbert, and he was dead.

"Man, looks like he just got himself killed by that pickup truck. Must have walked right out in front of him. Cracked that guy's windshield…"

Emily didn't hear the rest of Wayne's description of the accident scene.

"Just get me to the airport, please," Emily said firmly.

She didn't look back. She didn't feel sorrow. She didn't feel pain. She felt nothing at all.

# Chapter Thirty-Four

EMILY SLID THE SOFT, pale beige eel skin pump off her slender foot. She gently rubbed the ball of her heel as she pointed her toes as far as they would reach, stretching her foot back and forth. This simple exercise had been passed down to her from a veteran politician's wife, and Emily was forever grateful that she had learned to master the technique. The process was simple, it didn't attract attention, and it gave immediate relief to her overworked arches.

"What I wouldn't give for a steaming hot bath and a pedicure," she mused quietly to herself. She sat up straight and stiffened her back, turning her head from side to side in an attempt to ease some of the built up tension from her aching body.

The Senate campaign had been a grueling, hard fought battle, but Marcus had prevailed as the victor. The last six years had been a dazzling array of dinners, campaigns, fights, victories, hand pumping, baby kissing, fund raising, and give and take. She often wondered why Marcus had run for the Senate after two successful runs for Congress. If he had desired a seat in the Senate, why had he run for Congress in the first place? And why had he waited so late in life to attempt a political career?

Of course, Emily already knew the answers to her questions. Abigail Shane. For some reason, Abigail thought Marcus must first pave his political career through the avenues of a legal career. And not just any legal career; he had to be the most sought after and highly paid attorney in the city of Seattle. Then, he needed a wife. Emily, of course, had finally filled the position. This, though, had sidelined Abigail's plans somewhat, because she had not hired Emily for the job. She had been thrown a curve ball when Marcus found his own wife all by himself. But, the elder Mrs. Shane had not been deterred. No, Emily indeed worked nicely into the scheme of things.

The run for Congress had merely been a stepping stone to test the political waters. The feisty matriarch hadn't wanted to move too quickly, yet she knew she didn't want or have time to waste either. Marcus was a machine with two quick victories, and then came a shocker of an announcement: he was running for the Senate.

Emily hung her head in quiet silence as she thought back to the headlines that had been the hot topic for months after the announcement. Free publicity. It had worked like a charm. Marcus was popular, and he was a huge success as a freshman Congressman. And when the time had come, who in their right political mind would have resisted running against Senator Fred Cummings, once his indiscretions, pay-offs, and misappropriations of federal funds had become public and he had been totally humiliated.

Perfect timing indeed, Emily thought. She wondered just how heavy a hand Abigail Shane had played in not only the disclosures of Senator Cumming's wrong doings, but in his wrong doings as well. Something else pulled at her from within. Call it woman's intuition, but Emily believed Abigail Shane had paid off others along the way to ensure Marcus's success. She shuddered at the thought that someday, when they least expected it, all of his mother's shady dealings would come back to haunt poor Marcus.

Emily carefully eyed Abigail as she worked the crowd. Abigail was smiling, as if she really cared and was interested in the person to whom she spoke. She gently laid her long spidery fingers on someone's forearm or shoulder.

"Nice maneuver," Emily thought. "Make the person feel special. Draw them into your web." Emily noticed how the older woman talked with a prefixed and pretentious glare while all the time scanning the room to find her next campaign contributor and victim.

"Senator Shane." It wasn't Marcus the older woman wanted as senator, but herself. Marcus was merely the only way for her to get there.

&#8766; ✳ &#8766;

SINCE HER HUSBAND WAS SWORN in just over a year ago, Emily's schedule had been literally nonstop. The trips back and forth to Washington, D.C. had been difficult on Emily and Marcus. His townhouse was lovely, but Emily still didn't feel comfortable living there. Marcus had insisted she stay in his home state of Washington with the children, and for the past year she hadn't argued. Her meetings, luncheons, speeches, and other engagements on behalf of him, as the "home representative"—as Marcus called her—had nearly tripled in the past months. She wondered if her twins even knew her these days.

She watched Marcus from across the room. He had been coming home more often and staying longer. He worked from his downtown office, but lately he had taken to working from out of the house in the large library and study. Watching him, she noticed how extremely tired and physically worn out he appeared. His eyes were a little sunken and his shoulders slumped. He definitely needed a rest.

She wasn't sure how he kept going on two and three hours of sleep each night, only to run a full schedule that started in the wee hours each day. She had a feeling it had to do with the pink pills, the yellow pills, or the green pills he consumed at an alarmingly increasing frequency. His mother had been the one to insist he take them. Emily thought back to the dinner party she had hosted just six months prior.


"HERE, MARCUS, TAKE THESE, darling. Dr. Stevens said they would help you rest tonight."

"No thank you, Mother. I've already had three Scotches and I really don't think…"

"Marcus, take these. They will help you sleep. Take them now. Go ahead. Don't be a fool, Marcus. You have to have rest when you can get it. If you have trouble in the morning and feel sluggish, Dr. Stevens said to simply take two of these and it will offset any side affects you may have from these." Abigail held up two pill bottles. One held the pills Marcus took each morning. In the other, she held the pills he took each evening.

She smiled warmly as she pressed the pills into Marcus's hand. Emily remembered staring at Marcus, wondering what the two of them were discussing. He had looked sad and lonely. He had looked defeated. Then she had seen him take the pills.

"WHAT MEDICATION WERE YOU taking tonight, Marcus?" Emily asked as they readied for bed.

"Oh, just something Mother asked me to take. Something to help me rest."

"Marcus, please be careful."

"I will Emily. Don't you start on me, too."

If only she had insisted that he not take them. Of course, she hadn't known at the time that he would start the cycle of taking sleeping pills at night and then stimulants each morning. Marcus was having a difficult time staying focused. Perhaps it was because he was dedicated to a fault.

Privately, he wanted to please his mother, but publicly, he wanted to please the masses. Deep down, he was torn between the two. He overemphasized every minute detail, creating more work for himself each day in the process. By trying so diligently to appease and please his mother, who was becoming more and more demanding, not only of his time but also of her personal requests for friends and associates, he was sacrificing his health, his time, and himself.

She, on the other hand, was a well oiled evil machine. Her personal contacts and paybacks caused Marcus a great deal of frustration and stress, and, Emily guessed, a considerable amount of soul searching, too. She knew Marcus wanted to do right. He had honestly run for Congress and then for the Senate to serve the people. It just turned out that he had to serve his mother first.

A COMMOTION AND THEN a woman's scream caused Emily to jerk her head in Marcus's direction. At that precise moment she saw Abigail glaring disdainfully toward the floor. Emily barely heard the clatter of comments flying around the room as she dashed to the other side of the banquet hall.

"Someone get a doctor."

"Oh dear, is he dead?"

"Where's Mrs. Shane?"

"I am right here you idiot."

"No, I meant Mrs. Shane. The Senator's wife."

Emily's heart was racing. There, lying face up was Marcus. His face was ashen and his lips were blue. His eyes were shut tightly, as if he didn't want to hear anything around him, but Emily knew he couldn't hear anything now. He was unconscious.


"YOU'RE GOING TO HAVE TO LAY off the pills. If you don't, Senator Shane, you will be dead. Not to mention your emotional health. This roller coaster of up and down will cause a severe depression to set in and you will have a terrible time shaking it."

"Don't be silly," his mother interrupted. "Senator Shane is not on any pills, and I direct you to omit any such thing from your medical charts. He is simply exhausted from work. Do I make myself clear?" she said icily.

"Perfectly. Senator Shane, I suggest you get some rest. Some honest rest, if you know what I mean. I will forward all of my information to Dr. Stevens when he returns from vacation," the young doctor said with an air of defiance as he strode from the room, loudly snapping the medical chart file shut.

"Young doctors. Think they know it all. Now, Marcus, I don't know what you were mixing and whatnot, but what you did is not acceptable. Now get some rest and I will have Sara come by in the morning." The elder Mrs. Shane left the room without giving her son any tenderness, maternal kindness, or any comfort at all.

Emily rose from the corner chair and walked softly to Marcus's side. She gently touched his forehead and stroked his eyebrows.

"Hey, fella. How are you feeling?"

Marcus managed a weak smile. Emily thought how powerless he looked at that particular moment.

"I love you, Marcus. If you need anything, I am right here. And when you are ready to talk about tonight, I will still be right here with you, and for you."

Marcus slowly nodded his head and let his heavy eyelids close, and for the first time in almost half a year, he slept an honest sleep as the young doctor had said. He slept without the aid of any pills, alcohol, or anything else, other than Emily by his side, gently holding his hand. Emily watched as he slept peacefully. She wondered if he had intentionally taken too many pills, and if he had let the alcohol and the drugs get out of control on purpose.

"Why, Marcus? Why?" she whispered. But, Emily knew the answer already. Marcus's demons were sent to him by his mother. That much she knew. How many demons and how powerful they were she didn't have a clue.

# Chapter Thirty-Five

MARCUS DID WELL FOR the first four months out of the hospital. He adjusted his schedule and lightened his load. He traveled less frequently to D.C., and Emily even noticed how he stood up to his mother a little better. She knew Marcus and his mother had a falling out, so to speak. He had become very angry with her and wouldn't even accept her calls for three days.

"I don't care what she says. Tell her I am unavailable to speak at this moment," he had yelled at his secretary yesterday. It had to be something major, Emily thought. She decided it was time she found out what had caused the problem.

Knowing Marcus would never share this with her, she thought it best to try to find out what she could on her own.

Slipping quietly into his study, Emily took her diamond earring from her ear. She wrapped her fingers around it while she quickly leafed through the papers on his desk. She tried to open the bottom drawer of his filing cabinet but it was locked. Rummaging through the desk, she found the key taped underneath the panel of the first drawer. Emily's heart raced. She felt like a thief in her own home. She knew whatever it was that had made him angry with his mother would be in his home. He wouldn't dare leave it in his office for anyone else to see or be exposed to. Marcus may have been angry with his mother, but he was also securely tied to her, and was very protective of her.

Emily opened the cabinet drawer and began shuffling through the files and papers. "Bingo!" Emily said under her breath. There it was. She knew as soon as she saw the file that it was the answer to many of her questions. Wallace and Sons Contractor's file was dog-eared, as if someone had gone through it a thousand times. Emily quickly perused its contents. It quickly became crystal clear to her. His mother had insisted that he give Wallace and Sons state contracts and backing and that he push them through on several large state and federal projects when they were clearly not the lowest bidder. But on each occasion, their bid had been changed and they always became the lowest bidder.

Emily also remembered the close family connection the elder Wallace had with Abigail Shane. The world may not have known this and the good people of Washington State evidently didn't know it, but Emily did. Carefully replacing the file to its original position, Emily spotted another file that made her gasp. The file behind it was marked "Robby Brooks."

"Why on earth would Marcus have a file on Robby?"

With shaking hands, Emily took the file from its resting place. She seated herself and swallowed hard. Was Robby doing something illegal with Marcus? Did Marcus have something on Robby?

The sound of the maid entering the outer room interrupted her thoughts, and in one swift and fluid motion, Emily returned the folder to its proper place, shut and locked the cabinet file drawer, and plopped down into the soft leather swivel chair at the exact time the maid opened the large pocket door of the inner office.

"I'm sorry, Madame. I didn't know you were in here."

"Oh, just looking for my earring, which I just found. Thank you." Emily smiled warmly while she placed the key back in its hidden compartment, securing it with tape as she chatted with the old woman. "I take these off because they hurt my ears, and I end up just laying them down. I remembered taking a call in here yesterday," Emily droned on.

The maid could have cared less. She had work to do, but she smiled politely and let Emily rattle on.

"Thank you. Now, please excuse me." Emily briskly walked from the room. Her heart was pounding. Her hands trembled. She took a deep long breath. She had solved one mystery only to open up another one. One she didn't know how to solve. She would have to get into the office again, but deep inside of her, she knew she didn't want to know if Robby was on the take or involved in something illegal.

"Perhaps illegal contributions to Marcus's campaign," Emily said, as her mind raced through the many possibilities.

"Okay, Emily, don't assume the worse until you have more answers," she repeated, as she made her way down the empty marble hallway of the house.

IF THE FIRST FOUR MONTHS HAD been good to Marcus and his recovery, the last two had taken their toll. Marcus was back on sleeping pills at night and stimulants almost daily. Dark circles formed under his eyes. He was irritable and any joy he used to have in his job or his life was quickly fading.

Emily heard him talking softly in the children's room. She knew he must be visiting Steven James.

"Now, you stay as sweet and precious as you are now. You hear me? And always know something. I might not show it but I do love you. I love you very much," he said softly.

Emily rested her head against the wall and closed the bedroom door so Marcus wouldn't know she had heard him. She listened as he walked from the nursery and followed his footsteps on the stairs. She slipped into the nursery and found Caroline sleeping peacefully. He had been speaking to Caroline. Emily was trying to absorb this as the nanny, Mrs. Watson, walked in holding Steven James.

"Good morning, Madame. Had a little accident but all is well now. Ok, Mr. Steven James. Into bed you go like the sleeping princess."

Emily was deeply touched by Marcus's loving words to his daughter, words that he hardly ever acknowledged. But, for some reason, his tender words were also deeply troubling.

"MARCUS, YOU DON'T NEED TO attend every single senate vote. You're traveling back and forth to Washington far more than you need to. I need you here." His mother's voice seeped through the thick walls.

Emily stood patiently outside the door, listening.

"Is it because of Sara that you want to stay in Washington as much as you do? I know Senators who serve and still spend an enormous time in their home state."

"First of all, Mother, I am a Senator. My job is in Washington, D.C. It has nothing to do with Sara. My colleagues are already starting to talk about the time I spend away from the hill. It is only a matter of time before my constituents do as well. I have two important bills up for consideration. I wish you would understand that this is not about you and it is not about me, or Sara, for that matter. It is about what is right."

Emily hadn't heard much of the conversation, but enough important bits and pieces had filtered through the pocket doors of the study. She had definitely heard enough.

"Sara. Of course. Why hadn't I seen that coming? Coming? No, not coming, but going on. For what, five years? Six?"

Emily was lost in her thoughts when Abigail slipped out through the heavy mahogany doors.

"Oh, Emily, do make yourself useful. Listening at doorways is so unflattering."

The cold words were worse than a slap across the face. Emily didn't have a retort. She simply stared blankly at her and watched how her lips were beginning to curl in a downward position, especially when she talked. Emily noticed that her appearance had changed over the last year. Her mean spirit was actually beginning to show on her face.

"Well, now that you mention it, Abigail, I do have things to do. Like move to Washington to be with my husband so he can better serve his state."

Emily had not a clue where that particular idea had sprung from, but once she had spoken the words, they made perfect sense to her. Although she was taken aback and was probably more surprised than Abigail, the total shock that registered on the old woman's face was worth it all. Emily actually heard Abigail suck in a breath of air. It was in that moment that Emily knew she had made the right choice. If not the right choice for herself and the children, at least she knew it was the right choice for Marcus.

꽃

"NO, EMILY. MOVING TO Washington is a stupid idea. I don't want the children there. They belong here in their home. With you and the things they are familiar with."

"Marcus, the twins are five years old. This can be a wonderful learning and growing experience for them. Please, Marcus. Let's just give it a try. You need to be there. You are so torn. Please," she said quietly.

Emily knew it would be difficult for Marcus to change his lifestyle. Especially if he and Sara had been having the intense relationship she feared.

Sara had moved to Washington, D.C. immediately following the election. It had just never occurred to Emily that Sara was more than a loyal employee. Looking back, she realized how incredibly naive and stupid she had been.

Besides, it was obvious that Marcus needed her. He needed help. The drugs were taking over his personality once again, and if he wasn't careful, they would destroy him. Sara wasn't taking care of him. No, he needed Emily for that job, because Emily was the one person who truly cared for him.

"Okay. But let's spend New Year's here and then move you all after the first of the year."

"Thank you, Marcus. I know the coming year will be good for all of us."

"Yes, Emily. The coming year will be a remarkable year. It will be good for all of us."

# Chapter Thirty-Six

"HELLO, MOTHER. YOU WILL never guess what I am going to do," Emily enthused in an excited tone.

The upcoming move was becoming more tangible for her, and with each passing day, as the big event neared, Emily found herself becoming more and more excited. She was even excited about the prospect of being closer to her mother. Now, perhaps the two could visit more often. Being on the same coast would certainly have its advantages.

"Mom, you can fly up to D.C. in a matter of hours."

"That does sound nice. Do you need any help moving?"

"No, moving is taken care of. It's all of the living details that seem to be bogging us down."

Emily and Marcus had finally agreed on her and the children staying at least six months out of the year in D.C. She would be making several return trips home for public engagements and previous commitments. After that had been settled, Marcus had become preoccupied and had turned the move completely over to Emily.

He had become even more withdrawn and subdued during the past four weeks. Emily assumed that it had to do with her moving to Washington, D.C., and the changes he would have to make concerning Sara. She also knew that his mother was furious that the family was moving away from her and her control. She had overheard Abigail berate Marcus on more than one occasion just after the decision had been made.

"Why does she need to be there? Tell me that."

"Because she is my wife, and most wives go where their husbands are,

Mother."

"Rubbish. Only a handful of Senators have their families there. And most of them are older. No, that little prissy just wants to keep tabs on you. She wants to control you. Mark my words. She will be nothing but trouble for you in D.C. You will miss having your freedom, Marcus. I know what you have been doing on the hill. Trust me. There is not much you have done that I don't know about. You will find that having wifey there will cramp your style."

"Mother, please. Give it a rest. I want Emily there. Why is that so hard for you to understand?"

Marcus grabbed his bottle of pills with shaking hands and dispensed three of them into the palm of his hand. He quickly poured himself a drink of fine whiskey, popped the small pink pills into his mouth, and threw back the drink, swallowing hard.

"Fine, Marcus. Have it your way. Why don't you take a few more of those little magic wonders and see what world you can live in for the rest of the day," she said sarcastically.

Emily returned her thoughts back to the conversation with her mother.

"Anyway, Mother, I want you to plan on spending the entire month of May with us. You know, D.C. will be beautiful in the spring. Promise me right now that you'll come."

"Wild horses couldn't keep me away. Are you sure I can't help?"

"Are you kidding? I've got most things cataloged and marked. We have packers and movers coming on the fifth of January. Marcus will return on the second and then Steven James, Caroline, and I will follow. We were able to get a morning flight and the movers will get there the following week. It will really be good, Mother, I just know it."

"Emily, you don't have to convince me. How is Marcus?"

She hesitated before answering. "Not so good. I don't know how to help him. I was hoping this move would in some way, I don't know, maybe give him courage."

"Give him time, Emily."

"I just hope he gives himself time, Mother."

☙ ❈ ❧

"MOMMY, WHAT ARE WE going to do for New Year's?" Steven James's big blue eyes, which were filled with excitement, peered up at Emily.

"Oh my. We are going to have sparklers and noisemakers and bubbly apple juice and stay up late and bang pots and pans at midnight. What do you think of that?"

Steven James burst into a fit of giggles as his mother ticked his tiny ribs, chasing him about the room.

"Where's that little sister of yours? Huh, big man? Where's Caroline?"

Through his giggles, Steven James continued running around the room, dodging his mother as he delighted in the game of "Try to Catch Me."

"She's with Daddy. He's reading to her in the book room."

Emily stopped in her tracks. She knew that for some odd reason Marcus turned to Caroline in his deepest times of misery. It was almost as if he wanted her forgiveness for something she didn't even know he needed forgiveness for. He would hold her and read to her and kiss her. And then, as if on cue, he would ignore her and pretend she was nonexistent when Steven James was in the room.

"Here, you start this puzzle and Mommy will be right back."

Emily quickly walked into the library. Sitting there on her father's lap, sleeping soundly, was her sweet Caroline. Her tattered baby blanket was tucked securely around the two of them. It was the picture perfect sight of security and happiness. Emily's heart felt full, and it ached briefly. She closed the door back silently. She would let the precious moment live on a little longer.

Something must be bothering Marcus terribly. She wished he would confide in her. And, she wished he would quit turning to the pills.


GRAY SKIES AND A LIGHT DRIZZLE greeted them on the morning of New Year's Eve. Emily stretched her long limbs and listened as her stomach growled. Pancakes and eggs and sausage. Perfect morning for the last day of the year. A day that will end the year and start new days to come, she thought.

"Marcus? Are you awake?" Emily yelled, but there was no answer. She rose and peeked into Marcus's bedroom area. His bed hadn't been slept in.

Emily assumed he had worked all night again, and that she would find him sleeping uncomfortably in his large leather swivel chair, mouth agape as she had so many nights before. She peered into the children's rooms. Steven James, her chronic late sleeper, was still sound asleep. His mouth, like his father's, was wide open. The covers were tossed to the floor. Emily covered him tightly and adjusted the shade to close out a sliver of morning light.

Tiptoeing into Caroline's room, she expected to find her watching TV. But her bed was empty. A quick fear ran through her, although it wasn't unusual for Caroline to be up and talking to the nanny or one of the cooks or maids downstairs. Caroline didn't have time for sleep. She needed to be up and dressed and doing something. Emily padded down the stairs. An uneasy feeling continued to grow in the pit of her stomach.

"Caroline? Caroline? Answer me. Where are you?"

Emily looked in the kitchen. The coffee was made, but the cook was not in there. She could tell breakfast had been started, but was in midstream of completion.

"Oh, good morning, Madame. I just had to get some extra flour from the downstairs pantry. Breakfast will be ready in about forty-five minutes."

"Have you seen Caroline?"

"No, Madame. I haven't. Isn't she in her room?"

Emily headed for the study and Marcus's office. Caroline seldom went into the study, because she usually got into trouble if she bothered her father there. The study was generally off limits to her, but not to her brother. For some reason, Caroline had accepted this as the norm long ago.

Emily slid the heavy door back. There in his swivel chair was Marcus. On his lap sat Caroline, pencil in hand, drawing on a piece of paper.

"Shh. Gotta be quiet, Mommy, or you'll wake up Daddy. He's still sleeping."

Emily froze. Time stood still. She could see herself from above. It must be an out of body experience she remembered thinking. Caroline looked up into her mother's eyes and smiled sweetly.

"Look, Mommy. I drew bells so we could ring in the New Year."

Marcus's skin was pale and taut against his cheekbones, but he looked blissfully peaceful.   Caroline had tucked her soft baby blanket close around his chest. His eyes were closed. His lips relaxed.

"I put my blanket on him because he was cold when I came in here this morning."

"Come on, honey. Let's let Daddy sleep." Emily picked up the child who reached up for her. She grabbed the empty pill bottle and slid it into her robe pocket. She turned to close the doors and looked back at Marcus sitting there so quietly.

"Oh, Marcus.  It would have all been okay. It really was going to be okay, Marcus. I love you," she whispered, as the tears fell silently down her cheeks. She closed the door and let her husband finally rest in peace. And rest in peace he would, thought Emily.

# Chapter Thirty-Seven

EMILY WAS COMPOSED AND self assured. She certainly knew she couldn't break down now. Not for her children and not for Marcus. She would remain strong and she would get through this as she had gotten through so much in her life. But this was different. She had people to watch over and people to protect.

As soon as the coroner left the study with Marcus's body, Emily asked to be left alone with no interruptions. She entered the study and locked the doors behind her. She moved directly and with determination to the top drawer and removed the hidden key. Then she opened the bottom file cabinet drawer. There she immediately removed the Wallace and Son's file. Her hand briefly touched on Robby's file. Instantly, she made the decision to take it as well.

She slid her fingers gently across his desk. Sitting in his chair, she lowered her head to the rich cool wood and rested her head in her own arms. There, she let herself cry. Her body shook from the intensity of her sobs. She heard her own screams and wounded heart cry out.

Emily didn't know how long she sat at Marcus's desk, letting her raw despair overcome her. She lifted her head and took a long, deep breath. A lot had to be done before the New Year would come. She had a funeral to plan. She had her husband's reputation to claim and an overdose to hide. She took the pill bottle she had hidden in her pocket and turned it over and over in the palm of her hand. No autopsy would be performed and he would be cremated before dawn. She had made it very clear that her orders were to be followed. She smiled slightly through her tears and pain. "I guess power used in the right way is a good thing, Marcus. Don't worry. Your secrets are safe with me."

Emily rose, taking the file folders and tucking them under her arm. She walked from the room with her head held high. Although she felt the weight of the world on her shoulders, a strange lightness was in her step, as she closed the heavy pocket door behind her, sealing the mysteries and secrets with it.

The doorbell sounded again. Dozens of people from friends, colleagues, and the curious to the press had come by the house within hours after Marcus's death to pay their respects. Emily had remained upstairs with the children and asked the servants to turn everyone away. A memorial would be held in due time. Until then, no comments would be issued.

"Thank you for your condolences. The family appreciates your sympathy and concern" had been the official release. She heard the familiar voice as it rose up the stairway and reached her.

"Emily!"

Emily put Caroline down and opened the door. Looking down from the balcony, she saw him standing there. It had been more than five years since she had seen him. His hair had specks of gray through it and gray edged the sides. He was a few pounds heavier and tanned. His face bore lines of concern. He held a bottle of champagne in his hands.

"Emily, I didn't know. I just arrived from skiing in Switzerland and somewhere over the Atlantic yesterday, I decided I didn't want another year to pass without seeing you. So, I stopped by to wish you and Marcus and the twins a Happy New Year. I am so sorry. Is there anything I can do?"

"No, Robby. There isn't anything anyone can do. Thank you."

"Emily, please."

"No, Robby. But thank you. It's nice to see you, too." Emily turned and walked back into Caroline's room and shut the door.

# Chapter Thirty-Eight

MARCUS'S DEATH SIX MONTHS earlier had taken a great toll on Emily. Fortunately, her mother had once again come to her rescue. Marjorie had helped to organize the elaborate yet tasteful memorial service that had been attended by almost one thousand people. Emily looked through the cards and letters of support once again. She found odd comfort in all of them. She studied the kind comments and personal notes people had written to her following Marcus's heart attack.

Abigail interrupted her quiet time when she slammed the front door.

"Emily, it's time we talk. Steven James will be starting school and I have just learned you withdrew him from the Country Day School. Well, I am here to inform you that I have pulled some strings and he is back on the roster. Now, I really don't care what you do with Caroline. Marcus's primary interest was to shape Steven James to take over in his footsteps and I intend to do just that. Beginning in August, Steven James will be staying with me fulltime. I have hired a fulltime assistant to attend to his needs. I would, of course, like to see Caroline. I will have Rodney pick her up for Wednesday dinners on a weekly basis. She will also spend every other weekend with me."

Emily looked at her, amused.

"Well, you've been very busy Abigail. But that is not how things are going to work. Not now, not ever. So listen up. I do not intend to repeat myself. You will not take my son. You will not visit my daughter. If I decide you can ever spend time with them, it will be supervised visits with me present."

Abigail jerked her gloves off and opened her briefcase to present Emily with some documents.

"Oh you are a silly, stupid girl. You don't think I've come here just to tell you what I want to do. No, this is what I am going to do. My attorney has already drawn up papers stating that this would be in the children's best interest."

"Abigail, let me finish. I too have my own documents. I have the Wallace and Son's documents. Every single detail. Every single correspondence. Every single time your name was mentioned. Now, you can make a choice. You could go to jail, and you would definitely go to jail. I don't want to ruin Marcus's name, but I know what he would want me to do in order to protect his children from you. I will ruin his name if you leave me no choice. Of course, you can vanish and leave me and my children alone.

"Oh, and I also found Robby Brooks's file. The one where you tried your best to ruin him, his company, his father? You gave his ex-wife false information regarding his business and his contributions. You tried to frame him for contracts he not only did not get but wasn't even involved in. And his personal relationship with me? I found the letter you wrote on my behalf. You know the one. Where I quit and never wanted to see him again? And how about the one where you caused his father's business to almost go under, forcing him to have to leave this area. So, please, don't be a silly, stupid woman. Leave now, while I will let you leave. And Abigail, don't ever come back, unless you are invited."

Abigail Shane rose from her seat. She put her short white gloves back over her aged, spotted hands. She clutched her purse tightly and picked up her leather bound briefcase. She looked Emily directly in the eye.

"This is not over."

"Yes it is. This is a victory not only for me, Abigail, but for Marcus. He was very good in his recordkeeping."

# Chapter Thirty-Nine

"HI, MOM. WE MADE IT TO the airport. Our flight leaves in one hour. The kids are so excited. They can't believe we're going to Hawaii. I wish you had agreed to come. It would have been so much nicer with you."

"You three need the time to heal, Emily. I think it will do you good. And God knows you deserve it."

"Thanks, mom," Emily's voice trailed off as she followed a familiar head bopping through the busy airport terminal.

"Emily, are you still there?"

"Yes, Mother. I'm sorry. I just thought I saw someone I knew. Anyhow, you've got all of my numbers. I'll call you in a few days. Bye, Mother. I love you."

Emily glanced around again, surveying the crowd. Who had that been? She was sure she knew the person, if only from a distance. Oh well.

"Come on, guys, let's go get some ice cream before we board."


"HERE'S YOUR BOARDING PASS, sir. First class will be boarding in ten minutes. Is this a pleasure trip?" The slender redheaded ticket agent smiled and flirted with the handsome passenger.

"No. Wish it were. Just business as usual."

"Well, I hear all work and no play is not good," she said, giggling.

"I've heard that before. But this trip has been put off three times. This time I am making it to Paris if only for one meeting. Nothing is going to stop me today. Thanks."

"Well, we'll always be here when you get back," she answered, suggestively.

"Thanks. That's good to know. See you."

Robby grabbed his boarding pass and tucked it into his suit pocket. He had ten minutes before he had to board. He decided he had time for a quick stop at the snack bar. Airplane food always left him wanting more, even though he only flew in first class.

He would have recognized her from two miles. She looked beautiful and vulnerable and brave all at the same time. She was leaning over Steven James, wiping ice cream from his mouth. Caroline must have said something funny because Emily threw her head back and laughed with her children.

He couldn't take his eyes off of her. Here was a person he admired more than anyone he knew, yet he had been unable to tell her. He knew the truth about Abigail and the lies and the deceit and how she and Marcus had set about to destroy a perfectly innocent relationship between two friends. It was all because of politics.

Emily had needed him and he had allowed them to bully him into disappearing. He had allowed them to make him leave her alone. Well, he wasn't going to leave her alone again. She was right in front of him. This time he wasn't going to let anyone get in his way. This was the time to make things right. He didn't even realize he practically galloped from his gate to where she was kneeling with her children.

He reached in his pocket and pulled out a beautifully embroidered handkerchief.

"Here, let me help you with that."

Emily didn't move. Her hand froze on Steven James's messy lips. She didn't look up. She simply stayed still. Kneeling with one knee touching the floor, and her hand wiping her child's lip, she slowly turned and let her eyes meet his. Tears instantly welled up in them.

"Thank you, but I think I have it covered."

"No, you don't. See, you missed a spot right there." Robby bent down and wiped a chocolate smudge from the corner of the little boy's mouth.

Both children stood quietly by as the two adults stared at each other.

"Where are you going, Emily?"

"Hawaii."

"Really? Me, too. I have always wanted to see Hawaii this time of year."

Emily instantly fiddled with her locket.

"Pretty locket. I don't think I've seen it before. A heart. Is that your heart, Emily?"

"It was my grandmother's. My mother and father gave it to me for my wedding gift."

"It's truly lovely. It looks perfect on you."

"What do you want, Robby?

"I want you, Emily. I guess I have always wanted you. But, I play by the rules. You have given of yourself to so many people. I have had to be satisfied to just watch from afar. Oh, I've kept up. Now, I just want to make sure you finally find happiness. I want you to be blissfully happy. Something I think you deserve."

"I don't know if I can do that, Robby."

"Yes you can, Emily. Because, just like that locket around your neck, you can find it all in here." He gently tapped his own heart.

"You have love, right here, Emily. In your heart."

She fingered her heart locket and looked deep into his eyes. She closed them briefly as if remembering a lifetime of hurt and pain and love.

"I guess I could try that," she said, smiling. "But just not right now. The kids and I will be back in about three weeks. Why don't you call me and we'll talk."

"Fair enough. I'll walk you guys to your gate."

The four of them walked slowly toward the gate and toward a new beginning. One in which Emily was sure would fill her heart with joy and lead her to a life without secrets.

Printed in the United States
202787BV00003B/115-210/P